BEARDED LADIES

Kate Grenville was born in 1950 in Sydney. After obtaining her BA from Sydney University she worked in the film industry as an editor and assistant director. She spent the late 1970s living and travelling in Europe, and in 1980 moved to the USA where she obtained an MA from the University of Colorado. Her stories have been published in magazines and anthologies in England, USA and Australia, and in 1984 she won the Vogel/*Australia* award for her novel *Lilian's Story*. Her novel *Dreamhouse*, set in Italy, was published by UQP in 1986 to great critical acclaim. She has been awarded a writing grant and a writer's fellowship from the Literature Board of the Australia Council and is now working on a novel commissioned by the Bicentennial Authority.

KATE GRENVILLE

BEARDED LADIES

University of Queensland Press
ST LUCIA • LONDON • NEW YORK

First published 1984 by University of Queensland Press
Box 42, St Lucia, Queensland, Australia
Reprinted in paperback 1985, 1987

Typeset by University of Queensland Press
Printed in Australia by The Book Printer, Melbourne

Distributed in the UK and Europe by University of Queensland Press
Dunhams Lane, Letchworth, Herts. SG6 1LF England

Distributed in the USA and Canada by University of Queensland Press
250 Commercial Street, Manchester, NH 03101 USA

Cataloguing in Publication Data

National Library of Australia

Grenville, Kate, 1950— .
   Bearded ladies.

   I. Title.

A823'.3

British Library (data available)

Library of Congress

Grenville, Kate, 1950— .
   Bearded ladies.

   I. Title.
II. Series.

PR9619.3.G73B4   1984   823   83-26051

ISBN 0 7022 1716 6

Contents

For Isobel and Ken

Acknowledgments

Stories in this book have appeared, in different versions, in the following:

"The Space Between" in *Quadrant* (Aust.) and *Southerly* (Aust.); "Making Tracks" in *New Stories 6*, ed. Beryl Bainbridge (London: Hutchinson, 1981); "The Test Is, If They Drown" in *Quadrant* (Aust.) and *Canto* (USA); "Meeting the Folks" in *Southerly* (Aust.); "Junction" in *Paris-Metro* (France); "Having a Wonderful Time" in *Southerly* (Aust.); "Refractions" in *A Ream of Writers*, ed. Susan Yorke (Sydney: The Society of Women Writers, 1982); "No Such Thing as a Free Lunch" in *Eat it Alive* (USA); "Country Pleasures" in *Accessories* (USA).

The Space Between

The banana-shaped tourists lie in chairs by the swimming pool and stocky Tamil waiters on bare feet bring them drinks. The daring ones have ice. The manager himself has assured us that yes, the water for the ice is boiled. Boiled and then frozen. Oh yes yes. Boiled, of course boiled.

For myself I avoid the ice. It's not exactly that I don't believe him. But I prefer to smile and shake my head. No ice, thank you.

Outside the cool marble corridors of this palace-turned-hotel, beyond the graceful arches framing the sky, the streets of Madras are hot. Out there the sun is a solid weight on the top of the head, a heavy hand across the back of the neck, but beside the blue water of the swimming pool the sun has been domesticated by umbrellas and palm-leaf screens. Where the guests sit turning brown or scarlet, Madras is as far away as a travel book.

Here by the pool, under a blue umbrella, Mr and Mrs Partridge involve me in kindly conversation.

— Travelling alone are you? You don't find it a bit . . . ?

Mrs Partridge's crepey old face puckers as if encountering a bad smell.

— A bit, you know, unpleasant?

Mr Partridge tries to clarify his wife's query. He rubs a hand over his bald head, red from the sun, and says:

— You don't find that these chaps. Ah. They don't let their own women out on their own. Of course.

They're kindly folk who do their best to conjure up the girl in white frills who must be underneath my baggy shirts. They even have a go at a little matchmaking. Mrs Patridge leans in and murmurs while Mr Partridge stares off across the pool.

— Sandra dear, we were talking last night to the young man who's here with the tour. A very nice type of young man.

Her husband brings his stare back from the middle distance and speaks energetically.

— Nice group of people here. The McFarlands. The Burnetts. The Pruitt chap. Good company helps, doesn't it? In this heat?

Mrs Partridge nods and shows me the pink plastic of her gums.

— That's him. Ted Pruitt.

I've seen Ted here by the pool carefully browning himself like a chop on both sides. I've seen the way the water pools around his body on the cement and the way the hairs on his legs stay flattened to the skin even after they've dried. I've enjoyed watching the hairs on his legs, and the shell-pink soles of his feet, that the sun makes translucent. In the small of his back is a dark mole, pleasingly symmetrical, the kind that can turn into a cancer. I have avoided looking at his face, filled with too many teeth, too much flesh, eyes of too knowing a blue.

On cue, Ted appears at the edge of the pool. His muscular arms glint with ginger hairs as he hauls himself out. The water streams down his head and makes it as flat as a dog's. He flicks his head sideways and glittering drops land on the concrete. As I watch they evaporate into the dense sunshine.

— Ted, we were just talking about you, says Mrs Partridge. Come and meet Sandra.

He stands over me, blocking out the sun. I squint up at him, at his face invisible against the glaring sky.

— Hi. What was it again, Sandra?

— Sandy, actually.

He stands above me, legs apart, water running down his body and spreading in pools around his feet.

— Sandy? Used to know a bloke once called Sandy.

He runs a hand over his shoulders, where skeins of muscle lie side by side under the skin.

— I mean, no offence of course.

He gestures and grins and watches me under cover of rubbing his head with his towel. I see him looking at my baggy pants and shirt, and my face half-hidden under the hat. When he stands up to dry himself, the muscles of his chest flex as he rubs his back, and twinkling water is caught in the hairs of his curved thighs. He bulges heavily, thickly, unabashed, into the taut weight of stretched red nylon between his legs.

Mrs Partridge looks away as he rubs the water off his legs. Mr Partridge breaks the silence.

— I was just saying to Sandra . . . Sandy?

— Sandy.

— Ah. Just saying what a good bunch of people we've got here. Lucky, really.

Ted shakes water out of his ear.

— Too right.

He sits down, leaning back on his hands. I see his chest

3

gleam in the sun but have to look away from the red bulge offered towards me.

— You been going around on your own all this time?

— Yes. It's been a lot of fun.

My voice sounds prissy in my own ears.

— Yeah?

He doesn't quite close his mouth after the word, so I can see blood-pink inner lip.

— Why'd a good-looking chick like you want to get around on your own?

He stares at me, waiting for an answer, but although I wet my lips with my tongue, I can't find one.

— You must have a bit of, you know, from the fellas.

He glances again at the shapeless pants and I wonder if he's thinking, on the other hand maybe she doesn't.

— Anyhow, any time you want to come around with us, just say the word. We'll look after you. No worries.

He smiles. It's the wide blank smile of a man who's looking down his own strong legs, safe in muscles and red nylon.

When the waiter comes over to pick up our glasses, I recognize him by the moustache, such a thin line on his upper lip that it might have been drawn with a ballpoint. Each morning this waiter brings my breakfast, knocking inaudibly before coming in immediately with his tray of pawpaw and the dazzling smile that makes his moustache go crooked. I put a hand over my half-finished drink and he bows. He wonders too, when he sees me each morning lying in splendour in the canopied bed, why I'm alone. His black eyes dart from Ted to me and he bows again before padding off. He shouts in Tamil across the pool to another waiter and their laughter echoes between the arches.

The Partridges excuse themselves. They walk off arm-in-

4

arm, slowly, like an advertisement for retirement. Ted and I sit in silence, and watch the waiter remove a toothpick from behind his ear and clean his fingernails with it. When he has finished, Ted sighs and says:

— Well, where you going next?

His voice seems very loud.

— I thought I might go to Bombay.

— Yeah? Look, we're all going there too, for the silver. Why don't you come with us? No good being on your own. For a girl especially.

He's watching me and I'm conscious of the size of his very white front teeth. His hair is starting to dry, fluffing out around his temples like down. I squint into the glare of light off the pool and picture myself diving in, trying to drown. Ted would rescue me, using the approved hair, chin or clothing carry to pull me to the side of the pool before administering artificial respiration. It would take determination to drown beside Ted.

— Well, thanks. But I don't think so.

Ted has not heard properly, shaking a last drop of water from his ear.

— Eh? That's settled then? We'll have a ball.

I have to raise my voice to say again:

— No. No, I don't think so. No.

Ted is in the middle of winking at me, thinking of the ball we'll have, when he understands that I have refused. The wink goes wrong and all the features of his face fight each other for a second. When they have resolved themselves into a coherent expression, it is one of suspicion and dislike.

— Okay. Suit yourself.

He gets up, flings his towel over the chair with a flourish, and dives in. He is a powerful swimmer, reaching the end of the pool in a few strokes and showing those pink soles in a flurry of water as he turns. He would hardly be able to imagine drowning.

— You've lost your young man!

Mr Partridge beams down at me. He and his wife are no longer arm-in-arm, but Mrs Partridge tweaks a thread off her husband's shoulder as he speaks. Behind the kindly uncle, winking at me from under white eyebrows, a sharp voice can almost be heard. *Some people just don't want to be helped.*

— We were counting on you to look after him!

Mrs Partridge's eyes disappear into a web of kindly wrinkles as she smiles teasingly. Behind the smile, embedded in the lines that pucker her mouth, is doubt. They both watch me, but I have nothing to tell them, and my smile is exhausting me.

Not far from the hotel, there is a cluster of shacks that squat in the dust, lining a path of beaten earth. Hens scatter under my feet and skeletal dogs run along nosing the ground. Pieces of cardboard cover the walls of the huts. DETER UPER WASH. They *are* the walls, I see when I look more closely. Women sit in the shade, picking over vegetables, while beside them their other sari hangs drying in the sun — tattered, dust-coloured with age, but washed. Is there another one in the dark interior of the hut? Is there, somewhere, the wedding sari, best quality cotton or maybe even silk, with the lucky elephant-border or the brocade border that reads GOOD LUCK GOOD LUCK GOOD LUCK all the way around the hem? As I pass, the women look up and stare, their lips drawn back to reveal stained teeth. They are not smiling, but only staring, and they look away when I smile.

Out of doorways a few small children appear, staring shyly, their huge dark eyes full of astonishment as they look at me. They curl one foot behind the other in embarrassment when I look at them and twist their bodies away as if fleeing, but their eyes never leave my face.

As I pass the huts the children drift out after me and at each hut more emerge. I can hear their feet padding in the dust behind me. When I turn around to smile they all stop in mid-stride. They all stare, motionless except for a hand somewhere scratching a melon-belly, a foot rubbing the back of a leg, a finger busy up a nostril.

On the fringes of the silent group the girls stand, curious but listless, holding babies on their hips. They stare blankly, shifting the baby from one hip to the other, automatically brushing away a fly.

At last one of the boys lets out a nervous giggle and the tension breaks. Suddenly they're all shrieking, dancing around me, bravely reaching out to dab my arm and springing back, squealing and giggling.

They seem to know a bit of English. They yell:

— Good morning! Good afternoon! Good night!

When I speak to them they explode and cover their mouths with their hands to keep so much laughing hidden. They don't point, but they nudge each other and gesture around themselves, miming my clothes. One boy, bigger than the rest, wearing only a tattered pair of shorts that hangs precariously under his round belly, sweeps his hands around and stands before us in baggy trousers and big shirt. He stares up at me and says:

— You boy or girl?

His voice does not prejudice the question one way or the other.

— Girl. I'm a girl.

7

He stares, not believing. After a moment he grins enormously and laughs in a theatrical way to show how well he understands the joke. Then doubt clouds his face. He ducks his head as if overwhelmed by his question, but pulls at my sleeve:

— You boy or girl?

He stares up at me waiting for the answer. His round head, under its short fur of hair, seems too large for his frail neck. He cranes up at me for the answer.

— Boy. I'm a boy. Like you.

He considers that, but after a moment of looking at the front of my shirt he bends over with laughter again. Now he's embarrassed and won't look at me. He says something to the other kids and they all stare at me. They're waiting for a proper answer. It's very quiet in this back lane. The horns of the taxis on the main road seem puny and very far away. It seems the kids could wait forever for an answer.

I start to walk back to the main road, but the kids follow, straggling after me along with the dogs and a hen or two. When I walk faster, some break into a run to keep up, even the girls, with the babies on their hips bouncing and crying. One by one they dart around in front of me and run backwards for a few yards to watch my face as they try again.

— You boy or girl? Boy or girl?

They're all doing it together so that the words have become a chant. Bah yo gel bah yo gel bah yo gel.

At the edge of the shack village they stop as if on a line drawn on the road. I walk on until finally I can wave good-bye before turning a corner that takes me out of sight. But they are still calling out even after I've disappeared. Bahyogel bahyogel. Their voices carry a long way down the quiet street.

Making Tracks

She takes her bag from him thinking he's never done anything like carry her bag before. This morning he won't even let her light her own cigarette. Buying her magazines, dusting the snow from her coat collar. Almost looking as if he might want to say Don't go.

She shows her ticket to the huge black man standing by the train, all navy-blue chest and shiny railway cap.

— All aboard now. Everyone just say goodbye now and get right on board.

— Yes okay thanks.

— Well

— Well

— I wish

— I hope

They kiss briefly.

— Well take care of yourself don't

— Have a good trip keep in touch

— Yes yes

— Well

— Well

Letters across a million miles, long and funny then short

and funny then just short. Letters every two weeks then letters every two months then a long silence. This time yesterday we. This time a week ago we. Let me see was it a month ago that we? That was back last year was it?

They kiss again. She rests her head on his sheepskin shoulder and he strokes her cheek with his.

— Okay. Bye.

She catches a last glimpse of him as she swings into the corridor. He looks thoughtful, as if trying to work something out. Portrait of a man bidding adieu to his mistress. He glances away down the train for a moment and in that moment she takes the step round the corner.

It's not too late. He's still there can't I go back?

Don't be dumb isn't one goodbye enough?

I can still change my mind I can still get off.

Why can't I go back?

I can't go back.

She sits in the dome car and waits for the imperceptible beginning of the long journey. There's no jolt, no whistle, no dramatic bustle. One moment the train is in Preston. The next it's not. That's all.

In that first revolution of the wheels on the frozen rail, as quiet and as irreversible as the melting of a snowflake, the whole round globe of the world comes between them. In that moment his face vanishes behind the glaze on snapshots, vanishes into three frozen glances out of frame.

She watches Preston passing slowly, these long grey streets where the snow has been trampled into slush, which for all their dreariness will still be there long after she's gone. She watches as the houses straggle away and the endless plains begin. She stares as if to memorize the billboards, the odd-shaped barn and the tiny triangular field, all part of the goodbye.

She thinks of that moment when her feet made the decision and took her around the corner. Now a great army of small incidents slowly — tiny footprints in the snow one by one — obliterates that moment. Already the decision is smudged beneath the imprint of the train moving, discussions with the porter about the bag, the bawling of the baby in the next compartment. Frankly it's a relief.

On the blank screen of the snowy plain outside she watches what happens when he glances up at the train and finds her gone, vanished in that second.

She's gone?

She's gone.

My God so fast she's gone.

Well she's gone. Pity it's got to be like that.

He walks back out of the station with perhaps one backward glance, past the counter where they had a coffee neither of them wanted, past the ticket counter where the machinery had started up with a courteous grinding of cogs, past the varnished benches, curved for some grotesque back, where they'd sat briefly.

He gets into the car and sits staring over the wheel with his hands still in his pockets before starting the engine and driving off rather fast.

But perhaps . . . does it have to be like that? She stares at the landscape where distance has disappeared, where near looks as close as far.

Perhaps he gets on the train in Preston, swinging up with

a crazy last-minute impulse as the carriages start to slide past. At this very moment he's making his way down the train, ashamed of himself but eager, looking in every compartment, checking every seat, closer and closer. Any moment now the door will open and he'll stand there with his hair hanging in his eyes.

Or . . . that blue car there, speeding along the freeway beside the train. It's his car, racing the train to the next stop, now ahead, now behind, held up for furious minutes at the level-crossing, horn blaring in rage, skidding at last into the station yard in Bullrose. No train. Despair. Train from Preston sir? Well sir that train's a good half-hour late, be along any time now. There'll be a noise at the door as she sits staring at the freight train alongside and there he'll be, huge in the doorway. I couldn't let you go.

Or perhaps the snow, now a white gauze over the plain, becomes heavier and heavier, a great dead weight of feathery snow blotting out the merciless straight lines of the tracks, drifting over the lines, piling up at the tunnels, making this unstoppable train pause and finally retreat (somehow) back down the line all the way to Preston. Amtrak regrets. Circumstances beyond our control. Probably an Act of God. All those billboards, barns, triangular fields ticked off one by one, goodbye forever becoming hello again, closer and closer to Preston where she'll call him up. You won't believe this, but . . .

They're all impossible. The chimera of choice. Nothing can change except by a different throw of the dice, or the finger pointing from the sky, that one we all wait for. Whose finger? Who cares.

The snow continues to seethe and shift across the plain and soften the brutal edges of the real. Someone's made a terrible mistake.

She sits and stares at the possible.

Absently he wanders through the house, looking around for signs of her presence. An odd sock perhaps. A third toothbrush in the rack. The house seems to have been wiped of every proof that she was ever there. But he keeps looking as if to find some message. He even casually looks through his pockets where she kept her hands warm, but pretending not to look, playing the absent-minded genius even when alone. Now let's see did I leave my whaddya-callit here?

At last he sits on the side of the bed. Mustn't forget to change the sheets. He smooths the cover slowly, like a caress. She's made the bed before she left. Nice kid.

He's surprised to feel tears prickling behind his eyes and goes to the bathroom mirror to watch this unusual thing happening to his body. His eyes as they stare back are red-rimmed, suffused, his face full and puffy. He lifts his eyebrows so the deep groove between them smooths out. The wrinkles everywhere have a more permanent look every time he examines them. He's getting old. After all he's old enough to be her father. Too corny for words.

It's easy to imagine the train's going backwards. All she has to do is change seats. Maybe with each roll of the wheels Preston is coming closer. Her mind greys over as the blown snow clouds the line between the wish and the action.

Sitting opposite her goodbye self, sitting in the hello again seat, she pretends it might be possible. Not for the

13

celestial finger to point and not for him to come anxious but glad to the door, but for me to act. Maybe if I think it's possible it's possible. Possible for example to get out at Bullrose and spend the night in the Station Hotel listening to heavy mountain boots crunching the snow under the window and the cracked clanging of the bell in the church tower. Get a ticket back to Preston and sit rehearsing what to say all the way back.

She leans forward eagerly to the window. Taking my life in my own hands. Phooey to fate. My problem is always I give up too easily. I wait for that finger pointing from the sky. Is this life's lesson — Your Own Finger Will Do?

Twenty-four hours seem to have left no mark on Preston. The waiting room is just the same and the varnished benches still haven't found anyone who fits them. She doesn't need to look around for the phones but goes straight over to them and knows before touching it how the receiver will be clammy in her hand.

— I was kind of hoping you'd come back, he says.

— I hoped you might be hoping that, she says.

The wires hum in the silence and she knows he's thinking as she is about how it's all impossible but she doesn't want to think about that right now. Sufficient to the day is the lunatic impossibility thereof. He's glad she's back and she's glad she's back. So far so good.

Now they've stepped off the straight lines they have to make it up as they go along. In the house with the snowy

14

darkness outside they're uncertain. Waiting for something, maybe a sign. They decide to go out. To celebrate.

What happens is, they nearly kill a girl in a blue anorak. He's driving very slowly — there's lots of ice on the road — but halfway down a straight street the car spins violently to the left and in a second it's swung back to the right, the nose leaps uphill, the whole car slides wheels locked across the road, rides the curb and finally stops within inches of pinning the girl in the anorak against a stone wall. He stops the motor and it's very still. Slowly he gets out.

— You okay?

— Yeah I'm okay. You need some snow studs mister.

— Yeah. Yeah. I'm glad you're okay. Can I, do you . . .

— I'm okay thanks. Thanks anyway.

They sit together in the car in the dark and she can feel him shaking although they're not touching. They say nothing but go back to the house. They light a fire and drink the last of the Scotch but in spite of the fire it gets colder and colder. At last he gets up and looks at the thermostat.

— This thing's way down. It's not turning on when it should. That's why we're cold. This thing must be fucked.

He stands for some minutes staring at the thermostat, then moves around the house holding up his hand to the air vents, not willing to believe that the rhythm of the furnace thundering into life from time to time, like the slow breathing of the house, could stop. Especially with snow on the ground outside.

— We'll have to snuggle up, he says.

He grins down at her trying hard to make it all seem okay.

— I'm scared we might die of exposure.

They don't die of exposure in fact at one point in the

night they get so hot the bedclothes fall on the floor. They make love to their invisible bodies and she wonders if he's such a silent lover with his wife as well. They go to sleep hanging on to each other. As if for certainty.

Next day the house is very cold. He phones the heating repair man and she hears him joking about the furnace choosing the coldest week of the year to break down. She hears him laugh and hears his fright.

The day's a blank and as full of sterile possibilities as the snowy plain. They touch each other often but silences happen and stay. The landscape can shape the day like cathedrals do for tourists so they decide to go and look at the mountains. The car at least will be warm.

They get into the car gladly to escape the house where things creak erratically as if some third person is moving in the next room. But the car is stuck in the ice in the yard. The wheels spin angrily and the car bucks backwards and forwards but it still can't escape. The neighbour appears to give them a push but it still can't get out. They all stand around and look at it and the neighbour suddenly says,

— Hey you got a flat here you know that?

They change the tyre and finally free the car and drive off.

— I haven't had a flat in this car for three years, he says without looking at her. Funny huh.

— A scream, she says.

At last they leave the town behind and drive higher and higher. The air is very thin and she finds she has to keep taking deep breaths. The snowy landscape blurs past, trees like hasty brush strokes on the revolving backdrop. She could have been travelling through this blank white land for minutes or years. She returns from a long way away when he says:

— Christ what is it now.

And becomes aware of a wheeeoooooeeeeooooo siren behind them and a cop waving them down. She feels a clutch of guilty panic and sees out of the corner of her eye how his shoulders are tense as he pulls the car over and stops, his hands blindly checking that he's put the handbrake on and the car's in neutral. She watches his hand on the gearstick, then reaching for the ignition key. He changes his mind and checks the handbrake again before the hand goes back to the key and switches it off.

— Hi officer, he says, getting out. What's the problem?

She hears only occasional words as they stand beside the car talking in reasonable tones. It appears that the vehicle's indicator system is operating defectively. The cop's face is impassive behind his dark glasses as he listens to the promises. Get it fixed just as soon as I get back to town, no won't yes officer yes no certainly sure sure.

When the cop has gone they sit for some time staring at the road ahead. She watches out of the corner of her eye as he carefully puts his driver's licence away in his wallet and puts the wallet in his pocket.

— Well.

He looks at her at last and tries to smile but his eyes slide away.

— Let's try again.

He drives very slowly now, even pulling over to let other cars pass. Wondering wooden faces gape out of the windows at them creeping along the smooth highway in the sharkshaped car. It's not a convertible but it's a sportscar, he's always at pains to point out.

He wants to take her to a particular spot he knows, where he implies they could have what he calls a cuddle. They turn off the highway onto a smaller road where the snow is piled up at the sides and there's less traffic. This road after a while becomes a thin strip of black between the snow banks and at last it's just a narrow icy strip of grey. He stops talking and she sees he's concentrating hard on not sliding on the ice.

— Not too far now, he says as if to himself.

The car is very silent. They haven't passed another car for half an hour and the landscape is empty of humanity. She sees him hunched forward over the wheel as he steers the car between the banks of snow. When they finally get to the place he had in mind he straightens up and looks at her.

— We made it.

He grins and kisses her but they feel uneasy kissing in this silent valley where the pine trees seem to stand and watch. He breaks away from the embrace and looks quickly over his shoulder. The trees stand on guard but out of the corner of her eye she keeps thinking she sees something move. When she looks at the spot there's nothing there. The day is fading and already this valley is in deep chill shadow. The nights here must be inhumanly cold she thinks and hopes the car doesn't get stuck again.

— Let's hope the car starts when we want to go, he says and laughs.

— We'd really have to snuggle up if we got stuck here.

He grins but can't meet her eye. She thinks of dying slowly, numbly, frozen, on the plastic car seat. Her feet already feel a little cold.

— Let's walk, he says. Get the circulation going.

She gets stiffly out of the car and looks up at the mountains closing them in, all around them. You'd have to have eyes like a fly she thinks, to look at the whole barricade, otherwise all you can see is one snapshot at a time and not the encircling form of the whole. To the west, the great jagged axes of the ridges are radiant with a halo of sunset-red blown snow, as if a pit of flames on the other side of the spine is allowing the tips of its fire to appear. It's beautiful and scary. What if some mad whim seized my mind, she thinks, and I found myself (like a sleepwalker waking up witless with fright on the skyscraper ledge) up there where the air is blood-coloured snow and death is certain?

The frozen lake they walk to is only a matter of yards from the picnic place where they parked. But as the first tree comes between them and the car, and the silence thins to the transparency of space, she feels a flush of warm fear blossom in the middle of her back. The mountains don't care, that's what they say.

The lake is yellow, frozen all over with thick gobs and ugly lumps of ill-looking ice. She stands a few feet from where the clean snow ends and the yellow ice begins, a yard of solid land between her and any possibility of water, but she's rooted to the spot with fear of falling in, of being impelled by some inner madness, obeying who knows what voice, to walk or even run, skipping, calling out like a crazy suicidal drunk, right into the middle of this lake and falling through the ice to the death of her nightmares.

— We can go a bit closer, he says. It's probably frozen solid, anyway.

He takes a few steps to the edge and puts one foot on the ice, sliding it round in small circles as if to smooth the rough surface. He leans forward for a moment and then steps back quickly.

— I bet you could walk right across, he says. It's frozen solid.

She turns her back on the lake as if it might hypnotize her. The snow-deadened pines are like girls lying without breathing in their narrow beds, hoping the footsteps outside will think there's no-one there and go away. The ringing mountains fall down to this central spot, their drifts and ridges and lines all pointing to this well containing a man, a woman, and a lake like a jaundiced eye.

— Let's go, he says.

— Let's go.

The car starts, though only on the third attempt, and in his haste to get back to the highway he drives a little faster than on the way in. They leave behind the basin under the guarding mountains and the country opens up a little. They drive in their cocoon, the snowy landscape dim now beyond the headlights.

They feel better with every mile they travel and she has her arm around his shoulder and his hand is on her thigh. Neither of them reacts quickly when something brown and blurry darts out of the side of the road and flashes for an instant in the headlights. There's a tiny jolt to the car and a soft thump as the body of some small animal splits with a soundless scream that she feels in the pit of her stomach.

— Oh no oh no oh no, she hears him moan as he pulls over and stops the car.

Without looking at her he gets out and she hears him running back up the road. She hears him slither once in his smooth-soled shoes on the ice and after a few moments she hears him coming back, slowly. She makes herself look at him although she feels sick. He's very pale and the muscles around his mouth are tense. He glances at her once then looks away.

— Is it dead?

— Yes. Yes. It's dead.

He starts the car again and takes off so fast the wheels spin and whine for a moment before they grip.

— Good and dead.

There's silence for a long time and she sees that he's driving as fast as he safely can, concentrating hard on driving as fast as possible so as not to think about anything. At last they reach the highway and he accelerates along the smoothly uncoiling ribbon of road. She sees his tense shoulders relax. He looks at her and smiles.

— Wow. I hate that. But it was a quick death.

He takes her hand.

— Hey don't look so bad about it, he says. It's okay.

She makes herself smile and he smiles back.

— It's okay, he says again.

— I'll leave tomorrow, she says.

He looks at her and then at the road in silence.

— I'm very fond of you you know that, he says at last.

— I'm very fond of you too, she says.

He touches her cheek quickly and then takes her hand and they sit holding hands tightly until they get to the house. It's beautifully warm. He goes around all the rooms holding his hand up to each vent to feel the warm breath restored.

— Looks like that guy came anyway. Let's hope it doesn't go out again.

The house is very quiet now and they sit together, arms around each other, staring into the fire.

She goes to the window and looks out. She'll never know what his yard looks like without its smooth cover of snow. It could be neatly paved with the corpses of young girls, their throats ritualistically slit and their staring eyes wide. Or gold bars from the bank. Or just grass. They'd all look the same under the snow.

— Let's go to bed huh, he says at last. Maybe the bogeyman won't get us there. If we get under the covers and you tell me a story about the little furry things in the trees.

They make love and he falls asleep straight away without waiting for a story about the little furry things in the trees. She stares wide-awake into the dark and finally slides out of bed to crouch in the living-room in front of the embers of the fire. She opens the curtains and moonlight streams in. She sits for a long time with her back to the fire, warm on one side and cool on the other, staring at the impassive snow outside. She has a feeling that if she waits long enough something will happen but nothing does.

When she wakes up it's very early and she sees that this is the time to go. He doesn't wake as she dresses and packs her bag. When she's finished, she stands in the middle of the room, feeling nothing and feeling terrible. The world's at a standstill. Goodbye again. She bends down to kiss him and his warm drowsy arms slide around her.

— Goodbye, she says. Look after yourself.

— See you later, he murmurs through sleep, and kisses her.

See you later she thinks emptily watching the landscape through the grimy window as the train is sucked streaming down through tunnels towards the sea. See you later.

The pine trees, valleys, cuttings, streams, more pine trees, flow past without change, circling around the train. The distant line of mountain ridges hardly moves, the slow outer rim of the wheel. Closer and closer towards the centre the trees move faster and faster, the nearest circling so fast their shapes blur. Finally they move so fast they stop moving, stilled in the hub: the space inside a carriage, a compartment, a head, hurtling on, motionless.

The Test Is, If They Drown

Miss Spear in number forty-two is a witch. From the street we can see her sometimes on her verandah, spreading her hair over a towel on her shoulders to dry in the sun. We gather at a safe distance and whisper across the sunny air — Witch! The hiss fades before it reaches her. She never looks around at us.

Behind her house, up on The Rock, my gang and Mick's gang meet. From high above we can look down into her garden, where the cat stalks among great clumps of vine-smothered rose bushes, and sometimes Miss Spear herself comes out and drags ineffectually at the consuming creepers.

Miss Spear is what happens to you if the orange peel doesn't make a letter when you drop it on the ground. It nearly always makes an S. That means you'll marry Steven or Sam or Stan. Sometimes it makes a C and you take a second look at Carl and Conrad. Miss Spear's what happens to you if you don't step on all the cracks in the footpath between the school gate and Spencer's shop. Miss Spear's what happens to you if the numbers on the bottom of the bus ticket don't add up to an even number. She's what happens when you lose a game of Old Maid.

When she leaves the house to shop, she wears a skirt that reaches her ankles, and sandshoes. She's never been seen without the unravelling straw hat with the feathers stuck in the band. The cat comes to the gate with her and sits with its front paws tidily together and its eyes narrowed waiting for her to come home.

Mum calls her *Poor Miss Spear*, and says there's a sad story there somewhere. Dad says that Miss Spear wasn't ever anything to write home about. Mum shakes her head and mashes the spuds with a great rattle, punishing them, her lips gone thin. She thumps the saucepan down on the table and says that it's a good thing Miss Spear's got her house and a bit of independence at least. Dad laughs as he pulls the potatoes towards him and says he reckons she's got a bob or two stashed away in there.

At the shops she buys fish and milk and according to Mr Spencer the grocer, more eggs than you'd believe. The butcher skilfully rolls the corned beef and ties it with string, living proof that no-one needs more than two fingers on each hand. He tells Mum that Miss Spear comes in once a month for a piece of best fillet. He doesn't see hide nor hair, he says, then regular as clockwork there she is wanting a bit of best fillet. The butcher says he supposes Old Spear's harmless, and Mum agrees with a sigh as she puts the corned beef in the basket.

Of course Miss Spear isn't really just an old maid whose dad left her the house when he died, like they say. She can't really be just an old stick whose cat gets fish every day while she makes do with eggs except for a treat once a month. An old lady wearing funny clothes living in a big house with a cat must be a witch. No way she can be anything else. A witch a murderer a gobbler of children a creature from another planet. An alien.

Up on The Rock we watch her cat stalking a butterfly through the long grass, sliding on its belly, ears flattened to its skull. My gang has just beaten Mick's gang at spitting. All us girls got it further than the boys. And in spite of her ladylike pucker, Sonia got it furthest of all.

Mick shifts round restlessly, looking for a way to impress us.

— Betchas don't know what she did, the Witch, he says. Betchas can't guess.

I lean back and pick a scab on my knee. I'm not worried, I can beat him at anything except indian wrestling and even then I can usually trick him into losing. I'm better at nearly everything than the boys. Pam and Sonia are hopeless the way they're always worried about getting dirty or being home late for tea. But they're my gang and I'm the only girl that's got one.

Mick hasn't done too well with the suspense so he hurries to the punch line.

— She murdered her mum. Got this carving knife see and chopped her in little bits.

Stewart and Ross are impressed. Ross wipes a fleck of saliva from the corner of his mouth and says avidly:

— Geez what she done with the bits eh Mick?

Mick hasn't thought that far.

— That's, um, a secret.

He purses his lips and pretends to be very interested in the way a bird is flying past above us.

— Aw come on Mick tell us tell us.

Pam and Sonia won't let him off the hook.

— Betcha don't know, come on tell us or that means you don't know.

An impressive pause from Mick. Stewart and Ross lean forward agog.

— She buried the bits in the garden. Right down there.

He points dramatically down into the tangles below.

— S'that all?

Pam and Sonia are openly contemptuous and even Ross and Stewart are disappointed. Mick's eyes dart around as he tries to come up with an embellishment. This is my moment.

— 'Fraid you've got it all wrong, I say casually.

They all look at me expectantly. Girl or no girl they know I always deliver the goods.

— It was her dad. She killed her dad.

Mick is beginning a shrug. Mum or dad, so what?

— With cyanide. One drop in his tea every day for six months. She mixed it with the sugar so when he put sugar in his tea he got the cyanide.

The awed silence seems to demand some more details.

— And then when he was dead . . . she stuffed him. Like Phar Lap. He's in a glass case in her bedroom. To keep the dust off.

Stewart's mouth is hanging open and he's breathing loudly through his nose as he always does when concentrating.

— Geez what a weirdo eh.

Mick jabs him with a sharp elbow and shouts:

— Oh yeah, sez who. You gunna believe a girl, fellas?

Stewart snaps his mouth shut like a carp and nods. But his eyes are still glassy with the idea of such a sweet and unsuspecting death.

Ross glances at Mick and mutters to me furtively:

— What did she stuff him with? She pull his brains out his nose like them Egyptians did? What she done with the guts?

I've got all the answers. But Mick's tired of having his thunder stolen.

— Shaddup stoopid, she doesn't know nuffin. What ja believe her for?

He hawks and spits the same way I've seen his father do.

— C'mon, I can't be bothered hanging round these sissy girls any more. C'mon gang, I've had it.

We sit in silence after they leave. Sonia blows a huge bubble with her gum and watches it cross-eyed before sucking it back in. She chews it and tucks it away in the corner of her mouth.

— That for real, she knocked off her dad? Howja know?

Leadership means having no fear of the next lie. I say immediately:

— I looked in the window. He's sitting up there in this glass case.

Pam stops sucking the end of her plait and tosses it back over her shoulder.

— He got clothes on? Or not?

She's watching me closely.

— Course he's got clothes on. His pyjamas.

— What colour, Sandy?

— Blue and white stripes.

Lies must always be switched truths. The glass case from the skeleton at the Museum. Dad's blue and white pyjamas.

Sonia blows a great flecked bubble and we all watch as it trembles, threatening to burst over her face. She deflates it masterfully and gets up.

— Time for tea.

Leadership is never being quite sure if they believe you.

— Oooaaah Sandy you've got all moss on your shorts, your Mum'll kill you.

Her smooth pink face expresses satisfaction at this.

Sometimes I hate girls.

I plan my raid carefully, and alone of course. Pam and Sonia would giggle at the wrong moment or get panicky about spiders. And although I almost believe now in the body and the glass case, I want to be alone when I make sure.

I watch from behind the oleander until Miss Spear comes out to go to the shops. She sets off without seeing me, her hair showing through the hole in the top of her hat. The cat slips through the bars of the gate and sits blinking. It yawns once and begins washing its ears.

I watch Miss Spear until she turns the corner, and wonder what she is. Women don't wear hats like that, that you can see hair through. Women don't wear sandshoes and no socks so their ankles show red and sinewy. And women don't chop the heads off dandelions with a stick as she's doing now. If Mrs Longman at school with her smooth chignon and her dainty handkerchiefs is a woman, where does that leave Miss Spear?

When she's disappeared I cross the road and pull aside a loose paling in the fence. I glance up and down the street before sliding through the hole and dragging the plank back into place behind me.

Straight away everything becomes terribly quiet. I can still hear the billycarts rattling down Bent Street, and a dog barking across the road, but all these sounds are very far away, and seem to fade as I stand listening, until I can only hear silence ringing in my ears. Miss Spear's garden has locked me into its stillness. Behind the thick bushes and the fence, the street is invisible and belongs to some other world. It may not even exist any more. A leaf gives me a fright, planing down suddenly onto my shoulder, and my gasp seems deafening. The windows of Miss Spear's house stare at me and the verandah gapes open-mouthed. The shadow of one of the tall chimneys lies over my feet and I step aside quickly. It's a few minutes before I can make myself tiptoe down the overgrown path towards the back of the house. Damp hydrangea bushes, as tall as I am, crowd over the path, holding out clammy flowers like brains. The leaves are as smooth as skin as I push through and some are heavy with the weight of snails glued to them. Sonia and Pam would be squealing by now.

In the back garden, the grass has not been cut for a long time, and blows in the breeze like wheat. I creep towards one of the windows on hands and knees, moving twigs out of the way so they won't snap noisily. I'm doing well, being very silent. I am feeling better about all this when a mild voice behind me says hello.

For a few mad seconds I think that if I stay quite still I won't be seen. My green sweater against the green grass, the famous chameleon girl.

— I thought you were a little dog at first.

Since the earth does not seem about to open and swallow me, I stand up. Miss Spear is holding a carton of eggs and a bottle of milk. I see her teeth as she smiles, and her eyes under the shadow of her hat. I can see freckles across the bridge of her nose and a small dark mole beside her mouth. I've never been so close to her before.

— Exploring?

I stand numbly, waiting for a miracle. No miracle occurs and she moves closer and says:

— You live down the street don't you? I've seen you around.

She watches me in a friendly way while I wonder if I

could pretend to be deaf and dumb. The cat comes and winds itself around her ankles, smoothing its tail along her shins.

— You want some milk, don't you. This is Augustus, she explains to me. He's greedy but he's good at catching mice. Augustus, say hello to our visitor.

She pushes her hat further back on her head so that I can see her whole face. It is a perfectly ordinary old face with wrinkles in all the usual places.

— I don't know your name, she says, and smiles so that the wrinkles deepen.

— Sandy, I hear myself say, and become hot in the face. It is too late now to pretend to be deaf and dumb.

— Sandy, that's a boy's name, she says. I've got a boy's name too.

She looks at my hat.

— Your hat's a bit like mine, she says. And we both collect feathers.

I pull the hat off my head and crush it between my hands. My hat is nothing like hers.

— I've got something you might like, she says. I never use it, but someone should have it. Won't you come in for a moment?

Even Mrs Longman would not be able to be more genteel.

— Perhaps you'd like a glass of milk.

Anyone would think it's quite normal to be a mad spinster in sandshoes. I follow her into a kitchen more or less like most kitchens and watch as she pours some milk into a saucer and gives it to Augustus. She pours a glass for me and I sit down and drink it while she rummages in a drawer. I glance around between sips, feeling congested by this situation. But in this kitchen there's a stove and a lino floor and a broom in the corner. Just the usual things.

— Here we are.

She hands me a penknife and I open all the blades and look at it. It's a very good one. It even has a tiny pair of scissors. When I've inspected it I become aware of her watching me. I hand it back to her, but she won't take it.

— No, she says, it's for you. It used to be mine when I was a tomboy like you.

I turn the knife over in my hands, feeling clumsy. My hands seem to be a few sizes too big and I feel that I'm breathing noisily. Here I am, sitting talking to Miss Spear the alien, drinking the milk of Miss Spear the poisoner, accepting a gift from the witch.

She takes the knife and attaches it to my belt.

— Look, you can clip it on here, she says. Then it won't get lost.

She sits across the table and with both hands carefully lifts her hat off her head. When she sees me watching, she wrinkles up her eyes at me.

— Sometimes I forget I've got it on, she says.

Augustus jumps into her lap and whisks her cheeks with his tail. She brushes the tail away as if it's tickling her, sneezes, and says:

— He's very affectionate. As you can see.

She strokes the cat and smiles through the swishing tail at me. I can hear a tap dripping in a sink. The sound is peaceful and I find myself relaxing. I unclip the knife and while I'm having another look at it, I try to frame some impossible question. How come you're so normal? I could ask, or: What's it like being a witch?

— It's great, I bring out at last. Thanks a lot Miss Spear.

She goes on stroking Augustus and smiling. I can't think of anything else to say. I want to go, yet I like it here. I want to find the others and tell them all about it, and yet I don't want to say anything to anyone about it. Miss Spear puts the cat down and gets up.

— Drop in any time. Next time I'll show you the tree house.

Out on the street, the proper standards resume their places. Miss Spear is loony. I take the knife off my belt and put it in my pocket. I keep it in my hand, but out of sight.

Mick has decided he wants to hear about the brains being pulled down the nostrils, after all. But now I don't want to tell him.

Stewart glows with righteous indignation.

— We oughter tell the cops about her. She oughter be locked up I reckon. Them shoes she wears and that old hat like a . . . bunch of weeds.

Ross nods energetically, and his eyes bulge more than usual as he says:

— She's not normal my mum says. Oughter be locked up in the loony bin.

Mick says loudly:

— My dad says what she needs is a good fuck.

We all stare, shocked and admiring. Sonia giggles behind her hand. Mick takes courage from this and calls down into Miss Spear's backyard: What you need is a good fuck. The hydrangea bushes shift in the breeze and I feel the knife in my pocket. Sonia beside me shrills out: Silly old witch, and Pam joins in: Witchy witchy ugly old witchy. Ross takes up the idea: Witchetty grub witchetty grub. Mick stares at me.

— What's up Sandy, you scared or summing?

I want to push him over the cliff, ram moss into his mouth, stab him to the heart.

— She's just an old bird. Leave her alone.

Sonia stares at me making her blue eyes very wide and surprised.

— Oh yeah? Since when? You gone potty or summing?

Pam grabs my hat.

— They'd make a good pair, look at this dirty old thing just like hers.

She stares, pretending to be frightened.

— She's turning into a witch, quick Sonia, look.

Sonia stares at me, her mouth in an artificial smile like the one Mrs Longman uses when she explains silkily how girls don't shout like that Sandra dear. Pam is staring at me too. I see them ready to tear me limb from limb. I look at the boys and see them too, waiting to pounce, waiting for me to go further and step out of line. Their eyes are like knives, like packs of snapping dogs, like slow poison, like sharp weapons raised to kill.

Miss Spear comes into her backyard and pulls at a few tendrils creeping over a rose bush. Mick nudges me.

— Go on, say something. I dare you.

They're all watching me and waiting. Leadership means falling into line. Miss Spear is directly underneath, her hair poking through the hole in her hat, Augustus following a few yards behind as she walks among the roses. I want to stab Mick and Sonia and Pam and rip the smiles off their faces. Or is it Miss Spear I want to stamp on and destroy? Below us, she looks small, weak, hateful. I want to crush her like an ant, to be part of the pack and hunt her down as she runs alone.

— Silly old witch, silly old witch, I yell.

My voice is carried away on the breeze. She doesn't look up. Behind me the others are chanting:

— Ugly old witch, silly old witch.

Sonia uses some imagination.

— Red white and blue, the boys love you.

She laughs so hard she begins to dribble. We take up the chant, laughing at Sonia's dribble and the way Miss Spear can't hear us. Mick yells:

— Come on beautiful, give us a kiss!

I'm laughing, or something, so hard the tears are running down my face and I can hardly breathe. I hear myself screaming:

— Nasty old witch, nasty old witch, I hate you!

The last words carry and she looks up at last. We all stare in silence across the air. I seem to be staring straight into her flecked hazel eyes. Mick nudges me.

— I dare you, tell her she needs a good fuck.

The tears rise in my throat and run down my cheeks and across the silent air I hear myself yell, yell straight into her eyes, see her face on a level with mine and see the freckles across her nose like mine and her smile as she says I was a tomboy like you are, I hear myself yell and see her face change across the distance as I screech, You need a good fuck, fucking witch, until my voice cracks, I see her look down and turn away and walk into the house.

It's very quiet. I look around for the others but they've already turned away. Sonia picks her way down the first part of the rocks and turns back to look up at me.

— You've got all dirt on your face, she says. You look real silly.

She turns away again and climbs down out of sight. Without looking at me, Pam follows her. Mick and his gang have already gone down the other way.

The hydrangeas, the house, the sky shudder and fracture and I stand with my hands in my pockets holding Miss Spear's knife and whispering, witch, ugly fucking old witch, until at last the tears clear and I see the garden again, and watch Augustus as he darts out from under a bush. He glances up and seems to meet my gaze for an accusing second before he slips across the grass to the verandah. The house closes smoothly behind him like water.

Blast Off

Oh hi he says and the thought's on his face:
So this is Ken's girl he likes them young.
Hello I say,
who is this cold-eyed poet
with his black silk shirt and his stalin moustache,
Hello Karl I say
then I'm marooned.

New book blah
when I was in blah I was talking to Name Name
and he said blah ha ha.
Gonna publish in June yap yap blah Name Name Name.
So I said blah and he said I like your stuff blah blah.
Interesting the way the stalin moustache doesn't move
when he talks.

Ken's looking eager.
Blah yeah yeah.
Oh yeah ha ha.
Really no kidding.
Listen. When I. Listen. I. When I. Listen.

Blah blah yeah yeah.
Laugh blah ha ha.
Sure oh sure.
When I was.
He said.
I said.
Blah.
But he doesn't have a hope against that stalin moustache.
Blah blah blah blah.
Blaaaaaaaaaaaaaaaaaah.

There's me I've got a headache.
There's Karl who's high as a kite on blah.
There's Ken who has been my lover
once or twice.

I take his hand
which feels unknown although he has been my lover
once or twice,
I want to seduce you I say.
Here? Now? he says.
Yes I say.
Okay, he grins, he doesn't think I mean it.
I go for his zip he sees I mean it
but what does she mean everyone thinks.
Does she mean a gang bang?
Karl has stopped making blah his eyes are empty.
I take off my clothes
and my headache goes away at once.
I take Ken to the couch
and we have a flappy floppy blah bang.
Karl doesn't know if he should watch or not.

Then Ken says, You want to fuck Karl?
And he thinks did she mean a gang bang
            he's twenty years younger than me
            he could be quite a stud
            this could be embarrassing
            fuck this stupid little bitch
But I shake my head no.

Ken says Wow you sure know when you're in Paris.
Karl laughs too loudly.
I smile and feel the wet spot on the couch.

What's everybody feel like doing
let's have a drink let's go
says Ken.
I stand up and stretch and ask Karl to hand me my dress.
Would you mind?
I can see without looking he's got a hard-on.
We walk down the street through the dogturds
and wet trickles tickling down my leg.

Ken says
I always get turned on seeing a woman with two men.
Well have a good look baby I think
cos this isn't any movie.
Or if it's a movie it's gonna be MY movie.
Dogs scatter the populace stares
it's a whole new concept in blah.

I sit on the worn plush in the bar and remember
I've got nothing on under my dress.
I think of all the French fannies
English fannies

little French balls
and pale American cocks
that have been here before it's like the United Nations.
History in the making.

Ken sits beside me and thinks
this crazy bitch is she gonna get us all arrested?
Karl is opposite
and there isn't much room under the table.
He reaches his hand up my leg
and I put my hand on Ken's crotch.
Maybe Ken is playing footsies with Karl.
Snake bites tail
man bites dog
the worm turns
and the bunny's away.

Blah blah
furthermore in reference to blah in terms of yap.
Lacking substance as a poet yah yah.
A certain uncertain tone mars the overall blah.
Yeah but she gave me a great blow job a year ago ha ha.
Blah blah. Blah.
Name Name.
Ha.

Karl is impressed with Karl
Ken is impressed with Ken.
Karl is impressed with Ken
Ken is impressed with Karl.
I'm getting a headache again.

Karl gets up to go to the john.

I get up to go to the john.
Ken doesn't get up.

I take a leak and when I come out of the cubicle
Karl is waiting for me with bloodshot eyes.
He backs me up against the wall and starts to grind
but I tell him I have to wash my hands.
He watches me and his eyes are bulging out of his pants.
He kisses me
and grabs my ass like he's driving a dodgem.
When I turn and walk out of his hands he can't believe it
he stands there staring in the middle of the ladies' toilet
with his tongue hanging on the floor.

It wasn't long so Ken wonders what's happening.
Either it was the fastest fuck of all time
or it wasn't a fuck.
What is this fucking girl doing?
When Karl comes back his eyebrows are wet
but he still looks hot.

It's getting tighter.
Yeah you remember
whatever happened to what's-her-name?
Great screw in a kitchen ha ha ha.
Blah my first book blah blah
Three thousand four hundred and eighty.
Coming all over the goddamn boots
tits half out the window.
Blah.
Blah blah blah.
Blah.

Their mouths hang open like an idiot's drool
as I get up and go.
I turn the first corner I come to
and laugh among the garbage cans
in the stink of old piss.
I want to write something obscene on the wall
but I keep walking and keep laughing.

It's cold between my legs
and my nipples rub against my dress.
I walk along a bridge and know I could blow it up
just by thinking about it.
I feel as high as the Eiffel Tower
with a bomb between my legs.

A leering Algerian comes towards me
in a flasher's flapping coat.
I can't watch I know what's going to happen.
I watch a flash of flop between his legs
and hear a wet hiss.
He tries to grab my tit.
I slap and miss and he goes away laughing.

A stupid little tart but man she gives a great blow job.
A bit of a fling.
Spring in Paris you know.

Rosalie's Folly

The voice slides into her sleep like smoke into the last room of the house until she wakes up. My darling, he mumbles, my sweetheart. She lies feeling his warmth beside her and listening to his sleeping voice. She can almost see his face in the dark but not quite and slides her hand gently over until it's resting on his head against the thinning curls. He worries lately about losing his hair but she always tells him she loves him anyway. Flinging out a warm arm that strikes her shoulder he grunts, almost awake. He breathes deeply and evenly, falling back with a sigh into his dream. Anna, he murmurs, Anna, yes yes oh yes.

At seven-thirty the alarm rings as it does every morning of the year except Saturdays Sundays and four weeks' annual leave. She gets out of bed and shivers as she does every morning of the year including Saturdays Sundays and four weeks' annual leave, and shakes Martin awake. He's a heavy sleeper. Seven thirty-three the kitchen. The kettle's on the stove the tea's in the teapot the toast's in the toaster all's right with the world. In the bathroom Martin shaves, always from left to right leaving the upper lip till last. The kettle boils toast leaps out of toaster the whole kitchen's jumping. Martin comes out of the bathroom with every trace of last night's stubble erased.

— Hi how are you this morning, he says rubbing a hand over his chin as if to check that every last hair is removed.

— Fine, she says, and you? Any good dreams?

He shakes his head and feels his lips as if they're swollen.

She puts the daily eggs in the water and watches the sand of the timer falling, first visibly then too fast to watch, into the bottom of the glass. She has a moment of panic as the last grains are sucked through the neck. Stop stop she wants to say, not yet!

— I think I had a dream . . . she says balancing the eggs in the egg-cups.

He taps the top of his egg too hard and the shell splinters down the side.

— Hmmm? Got the salt there?

He takes the salt and makes a neat pile on the side of the plate. She watches as he eats his egg, making sure the ratio of egg to toast is just right. She pours the milk into the cups before the tea, the way he likes it, and asks:

— Anything exciting going on at work?

She has to concentrate very hard on pouring the tea because of the way the lid of the teapot falls off.

— Exciting? Just the usual.

He spreads jam on his toast, going all the way to the crusts. He crunches loudly and stares at the tablecloth.

Her egg tastes sickly this morning and she pushes the plate away and drinks some tea. It's too hot and she scalds her lip. As she puts the mug down suddenly he looks up at her before going back to his breakfast. She watches him carefully redistributing a stray dab of butter. His voice seems very loud when he speaks through a mouthful of crumbs.

— This bread's not very good. Too brittle. Crumby.

She smiles at his face but it's turned away as he reaches for more jam.

— Okay, she says, I'll get rye next time.

She squeezes his hand which doesn't squeeze back.

— Hey, gives us a smile . . . ?

He glances at her and smiles briefly.

— Time to go, got to go.

He stands up and leans down to kiss her in the same movement.

— Have a good day. You feeling okay are you?

She stares at the debris of breakfast.

— Sure, I'm fine.

He shrugs into his coat and wraps the long scarf around his neck.

— Okay, he says. See you at six then.

She walks through the park on her way to the Tube, recognizing the regulars who are there every morning at the same time. There's the old woman rocking from one bowed leg to the other with a snuffling clot of hair on its leash beside her. One day it'll snuffle itself into extinction and she'll stand broken-hearted beside the small stone that says FIDO MY ONLY FRIEND. There's the man with a face like an iron mask with his Alsatian sniffing the breeze for something to tear apart. And there's the corduroy couple with the bounding English Sheep Dog that will wonder, in a year's time (when they decide he's earning enough for them to have the baby now) why they don't love him any more. She can set her watch by the brisk old man who walks three times around the perimeter of the park, scrupulously resisting the temptation to cut off the corners. By the left, wheel.

However, these days in spite of himself he does have to cheat on one corner. It's only taken a week of garbage strike for one corner of the park to become a huge pile of rubbish. The heap thrives on the rich leavings of all those people who agree it's a scandal the government should do something. Terrible isn't it just terrible, says Mrs Laundromat, stretching the cardigan further over her huge behind. They didn't oughter allow it, says the greengrocer with one finger under the scales as he weighs her lunchtime apple. Is werry bad werry bad, says Mrs Ramachandran in the corner shop where the mice dart in and out between the boxes. The pile grows furtively. At night she's seen surreptitious figures cross the grass and as if by accident let their bag of rubbish drop. Who me? She and Martin have said nothing to each other, but any day now it'll be their turn to add to the shameful pile. How will she look the greengrocer in the eye then as they tut-tut a pound of carrots please yes they shouldn't allow it? Not in *our* street. Not in *my* life.

She's always hated the Tube and that silent crowd streaming through the tunnels towards another day. She queues behind the same dandruff-scattered shoulders as every other morning and gets into the same carriage. As usual all the seats are taken. She thinks of Martin, at work by now, unwinding the scarf and hanging it on the hat-rack. Smiling hello to everyone, to all those welcoming morning faces in his office.

She glances around at the commuters and for a moment sees them with the clarity of nightmares. These faces, jammed close together, staring off aloofly as if over vast empty plains. These bodies swaying and bumping together and cringing from every touch. That woman there, with a face brutally blotched with a thousand dark freckles like a plague out of which she stares. This frozen pinstripe type reading his *Financial Times* with only the morsel of toilet paper stuck to a fresh shaving cut to show that blood flows in his veins. This whole silent rigid crowd, worrying about the pennies, the pension and job security. Being in love and wondering about those long blond hairs.

At Euston she changes trains and buys a paper as she does every morning from the old man who says the same thing every morning to her and to numberless nameless others, Cheers thanks love, as he takes the money and fumbles through his greasy pouch for change. He glances at her and says, Cheer up love it might never happen. She smiles weakly and takes the paper. MI5 DOUBLE AGENT TRAITOR says the headline. She crams her way through the crowds in the tunnel towards the other platform, driven by some urge to hurry hurry hurry. Arriving at the platform she finds herself panting but the compelling urgency doesn't lessen.

The faces in the carriage seem small and made of some waxy substance. All around her the headlines shout BETRAYAL I TRUSTED HIM COMPLETELY SAYS SPY BOSS. That bony yellow hand, it seems to be attached to my arm but none of it belongs to me. That sombre face outside the window why is it staring at me? IF THESE ALLEGATIONS ARE TRUE I AM ASTONISHED. No my dear, *you* are surprised, *I* am astonished.

In the tunnel the train slows and stops. The air is dense and suffocating like a weight on the head and the carriage bursts with silence while the waxwork commuters hold their breath. Beneath her, a man with a thin moustache is firmly unaware that the train has stopped, that the bomb has dropped, that we'll stay down here forever having to decide who'll eat whom because the rescue party will never come. He bites his lip and thinks hard about the crossword puzzle. Kind of mammal in five letters, last letter n. At the other end of the carriage someone says in a piercing whisper, Getting stuffy isn't it, and he coughs and makes a wild stab at the word. All around her, people read their newspapers as if Truth were engraved on them in letters of fire. Unfortunates without newspapers wind their watches or work out 764 multiplied by 375 in their heads.

The train jolts into motion and the commuters shuffle and cough. IF YOU CAN'T TRUST YOUR CLOSEST ASSOCIATE WHO CAN YOU TRUST? The train thunders into the station and the commuters thrust each other aside to get out as quickly as possible.

In her office the puny plants droop towards the window trying to remember what sunlight looks like. The fluorescent lights shrill their subliminal needle-hum through the air and the typewriter sits up at attention waiting to turn words into black-and-white certainties. The world is very simple and quite trustworthy when you take it one letter at a time. Just don't look around.

Mr Lynch comes out of the inner office and waves a pile of papers at her.

— Good morning how are you this morning, he says.

Oh I died in the night thanks and you?

— These are very urgent I'd like you to get straight onto them if you don't mind.

She takes the papers and sits down and starts to type as fast as she can. Her mind empties and she follows only the tap tap tap comma space tap tap tap. She works so fast that by lunchtime all the letters are lined up in their uniform shrouds and the IN tray is empty. Every pencil is in its jar and the stapler is lined up next to the liquid paper. An orgasm of elimination she thinks and has a sudden urge to speak to Martin. She calls his office. He went out an hour ago, the switchgirl drones. Didn't say where but he'll be out for the rest of the day can I tell him who called. She shakes her head although she knows the girl can't see her. Shakes her head and puts the receiver carefully back on its cradle.

Mr Lynch comes out in the nick of time with more letters and she types them with great speed.

Deqr Mr Mortimer
Dear Mr Moetimer
Deat Mr Nortimer
Dear me mortimer

Come on you're going too fast just slow down and don't panic.

Dear Mr Mortimer

She feels relieved with every clickety clack space clickety clack carriage return but when she takes the letter out she see she's put the carbon in the wrong way round and the back of the letter is a code of mirror writing. She stares around the office wondering what's going on. The Office Monotony Pad stares back at her and she has to look closely before it becomes again the Office Economy Pad. The directions for the telex machine appear to be Clown Copyright. I know that can't be right that just isn't right where has he gone?

She blinks hard to clear her vision and grips a pencil tightly and tells herself to breathe deeply it will all be perfectly simple in a minute. The pencil snaps and a piece lands at her feet. She stares at her foot next to the piece of pencil. It's just my foot. In its shoe. With a piece of this pencil I've just snapped. Nothing to worry about. And this, yes, this is my hand lying here on the desk, it's mine, I am all right and everything absolutely everything is one hundred per cent okay.

She dials home and sits gripping the receiver hard, listening to the ringing tone and reading about all the emergencies there's a phone for. Police Fire Ambulance. What about the other kinds? She hangs up and dials again a few minutes later maybe I dialled the wrong number. It still rings emptily. She puts the receiver down slowly, listening to the ringing sound until it's cut off. She's run out of letters to type but in a frenzy of activity she rolls paper into the typewriter and starts pounding away like someone whistling in the dark. qwertyuiop the quick brown fox jumps over the lazy turd.

She stops, overwhelmed by this little machine that makes words sit up and beg one at a time. She looks at the plants yearning with their last feeble strength towards the light and at the terrible tidiness of her desk.

Dear My Lunch,
    As I am not feeling very well I have gone home for the rest of the day

She looks at this and giggles until she runs out of air and breathes in, feeling her ribs jump and her stomach contract. She gets up clumsily and knocks over the jar of pencils but she doesn't look back she has to get out. The telex machine barks at her as she passes. She hits her hip against the door as she goes out and it tries to slam back and hit her. Pulling her coat on, she pushes past blindly but one sleeve has disappeared. Where is it where is it where is he?

The quiet streets spring at her. GROUP URGES PUBIC

50

PROBE a headline sniggers. The Venereal Heating Centre tries to take her by surprise. A bus roars past advertising Hell Tours and a man with a limp goes into an On-The-Spot Hell Bar. The drinkers outside the Punch of Grapes stare at her as she passes Fiend's House. Then there's the Cobra Hotel where the desk clerk sits under a neon sign that says DECEPTION.

She breaks into a run but her coat wraps itself around her legs and flaps in front trying to stop her. An old man stands in the middle of the pavement in front of her with his arms wide apart as if turning back a cow. Easy easy he smiles as she pushes past. A bus grinds along close to her ear with an ugly roar like the world crushing itself to bits.

At the mouth of the Tube she hesitates and wonders if she should go back to work after all. She keeps her eyes on the ground as she goes through the tunnels and down the steps and waits on the platform. When the train pulls in she thinks of throwing herself underneath. Sweat breaks out on her palms as the moment passes.

Although it's an earlier train than the one she usually takes it's still crowded. She clenches her fists in her pockets and fights the urge to grab the grey suit next to her and shake the padded shoulder until something snaps. Inside she feels a great wail building up and thinks how easy it would be to open a hole in her face and let it out. Aaaaaaaaaaaaaah. She licks her lips and stares woodenly at nothing but after a few minutes finds she's been forgetting to breathe. She takes a deep breath that turns into a yawn, huge, uncontrollable, her mouth opening wider and wider and the breath jerking into her chest in gasps. The grey suit glances at her with panic in his eyes and she knows he thinks that she's going to cry. She covers the yawn with her hand and stares him down.

The park near home looks strange and she tells herself it's because she's never seen the garbage heap at this time of day before. It gleams triumphantly in the shafts of sun, a lavish harlequin lily among the demure trees and grass. A puny fence at one side has been flattened by its sprawling weight and the bus-shelter is engaged in intricate embrace with a tangle of wallpaper. The pile is already bigger than it was this morning, engorged with more furtive bags. Even as she watches a man comes over to it and shamelessly throws his garbage onto the heap. One bag bursts in the ecstasy of its flight and rubbish sprays out like confetti.

On the edges of the heap the vultures are already starting to scavenge, the parasites on this vast bloated whore lounging at ease in the park. People swarm all over it or stand chatting, holding picture frames and cracked plates. An old man picks out bottles and lays them together with palsied laborious care. Mrs Laundromat stands legs astride holding a stool by one leg like a doll. Funny what people throw out she agrees with the greengrocer who shows her his booty. You know how much these pliers cost in a shop? Good brand this.

She walks up the front steps reluctantly, but there seems nowhere else to go. Sitting curled up in the big armchair she watches the hands of the clock move around to six o'clock. She doesn't know what she's going to say and can't decide whether she'd rather be crazy or sane.

The clock strikes the hour and there's his key scratching at the lock. She hears him come in and stand inside the front door listening to the silent house. She holds her breath. He takes an uncertain step forward as if into darkness and stops again. The dense silence hums in her ears.

— Ah . . . Rosalie? You home?

— I'm here.

She hears him move towards the living room.

— It's okay I know all about Anna.

He stops and there's another long silence before he appears at the door and stares at her. Slowly, his eyes never leaving her face, he unwinds his scarf and sits opposite her, folding and refolding it. He waits. Oh my god oh my god so this is how it happens she thinks. There's no way out nothing to be done no escape too late now. She watches his hands smoothing the scarf on his knee as he waits for her to speak.

A Summer Aunt

Words arrive every once in a while from Mother and Father and Eve. They all seem as remote from me as the beaming brown natives in Aunt Naomi's books. *All well here but still waiting for the Wet*, Father's notes tell me, telegraphically as if even in a letter words cost money. *Bluey has got a striped pup*, Evie says in her beginner's slope-card writing, and there is a picture in the margin of something striped that looks like a sock, but must be Bluey's pup. Mother's letters are full of how the Flying Doctor had to come for the Asquiths at Budgeree Creek, and how the sickly Malone boy is recuperating at Manly. *That sea air will be doing you both a power of good*, her tidy pale-blue ink hopes. Her letters always end with a reminder that if I have any problems with anything, Aunt Naomi would be only too pleased to help. Even through the pale-blue ink I hear her voice sink to that strained whisper that means, any little female problems, you know, Louise.

Aunt Naomi and I are getting on like a house on fire, I have heard her telling people. *My niece Louise from the outback*, she introduces me, and holds my shoulder while I shake hands with a neighbour or someone from the University.

She is sweet sixteen and down here for the ozone, she adds, and everyone laughs.

On previous visits, Aunt Naomi was an alarming woman with glasses, whom the neighbours called *Professor*, and who had written books called **Present-Day Taboo Patterns Among the Hakadu,** and **Aro-Aro Kinship Structure.** These days Aunt Naomi and I get on much better. She can still be alarming in her glasses, but without them she is an energetic woman of no particular age, who likes to cheat at Monopoly on rainy afternoons. She has a well-tended smooth face, with one neat crease between her eyebrows — from too much reading, she says — and she dresses with care, in dark colours with vivid scarves. She was married once, and there is a photograph, and a gold ring on her finger to prove it, but Chester has been dead for many years. *I am a merry widow,* she says sometimes, and winks at me. *It is more fun to have a niece than a husband,* she says, and we laugh together.

At mealtimes she is serious, and discusses with me the fundamental evil of Man, and she is full of examples of brown-skinned depravity from her studies. Her assumption that I am familiar with all this, and agree with her, makes me feel very mature and very wise. Of course, I never argue. *Man is a creature of perversity and bad habits,* she declares, and I nod. *Man is ruthless and without scruples,* she says, and I am sure she is right. At the end of each meal I stare at the chop bone on my plate as Aunt Naomi reaches in triumph for more salad. But when I am thoroughly convinced that it's hardly worth going on, since Man is such a bundle of weaknesses, she pulls me towards her as I lean down to take her plate. *Never mind me, darling,* she says. *I'm just an old cynic.* I smell her *Chaleur* and feel her hair brushing my cheek. Close to my ear, her breath fills my head with noise.

We manage well in the house. Cooking together, we've worked out meals I'll miss when I go back to Mother's legs of lamb and roast chook with stuffing. But it would be impossible to explain to her just how to make our *Spaghetti Fantastico* or our *Steak à la Louise*. She'd try to make them, but somehow it wouldn't taste right. Aunt Naomi and I have worked out a routine for doing the dishes that makes it seem fun, and we take it in turns to vacuum the house. On Saturday mornings we sort the laundry and put it in the machine. I have a little pile of things to be washed by hand, but often, when I come back to do them, they're already washed and hanging up, dripping into the tub — the panties, the stockings, the bras. Aunt Naomi shrugs and smiles when I thank her. *My pleasure, darling.*

Although her house is enormous, we don't seem to have quite enough room. At the weekends, when I sit writing my dutiful letters to Mother and Father, and drawing pictures of things for Evie, I can hear her rustling through piles of brittle newspapers in her room. I write as quickly as I can, to finish my letters and go across the road to Cheryl's place and rollerskate on her driveway, but I find it hard to concentrate, listening for the occasional sound of scissors through paper as Aunt Naomi cuts out another example for her book. She has told me what it is about, but so many technical words confused me. She has collected a lot of material for it. The shelves of her room are loaded with clippings, and the floor is stacked with yellowing copies of a smudged and undersized newspaper called the **Voolalu Courier**. She doesn't like me to go into her room, and covers the clippings on her desk with her hands when I knock at the door and speak to her. *What is it, darling, these will all blow about*, she says, and looks at me awkwardly over her shoulder while she covers the clippings.

On previous visits, when Mother and Father and Evie were here, Father always cut her off short if she started to talk about her natives. *Now Naomi*, he would say, *we don't want to hear about all that, not at the table thank you*. But I like watching her talk about it. *These folk*, she says, slicing her steak vigorously, *they'll screw anything in sight. I was reading just now where a father of twelve was doing it with a goat, can you believe*. She laughs. *The taboos are quite different*. She pops a big piece of meat into her mouth and chews hard. *You'd wonder how they'd find a way*.

Her presence dominates the bathroom. At home, the bathroom is the most impersonal room in the house, every sign of human use scrubbed off and hidden away. But Aunt Naomi's bathroom is full of the smell of her *Chaleur*, and her strong black hairs cover the soap. Her creams and sprays and tweezers are not hidden in cupboards, but are piled on the window-sill so that I can examine them. *For my ears*, she explains when I pick up her depilatory cream, and she shows me the hair that sprouts on her lobes. *For my moustache*, she says of the peroxide, and she smooths her upper lip, where there is no moustache at all that I can see.

She gives me some money and even promises me a little wine. *Get something really pretty, darling*, she says. *You're only sixteen once*. She ruffles my hair. *Get something dainty, Louise, something feminine*. It takes all day, and seven different shops, to find the right dress. *For someone a bit special*, asks the shoplady with a wink, *a special date, dear?* Finally there is a yellow dress with a low neck that looks perfect, and just what Aunt Naomi will like, but at home I'm no longer sure and try it on in front of the mirror with my new shoes, standing and walking and turning so the skirt fills. The neckline is lower than any of my other dresses. I try out long serious looks, chin on hand, and see if my coral beads go with the dress. I wish I had a cleavage.

The night of my birthday, we both take a long while getting ready. Aunt Naomi sings "Daisy, Daisy", in the shower and the splashing goes on for a long time. The new dress, carefully pressed, lies across the bed with its skirt belled out. My best underwear with the lace, and the slightly too-high shoes, make me feel very womanly. With the coral necklace on, I stand looking at myself in the mirror, wearing everything but the dress. Or, looked at another way, wearing only my underwear.

As I come slowly down the stairs, one hand on the banister, I feel the skirt puff forward at each step toward where Aunt Naomi waits for me at the bottom, smiling up. She's wearing the striped scarf I gave her for Christmas, with her best navy, and she has taken off her glasses. *You're exquisite, darling*, she exclaims. She holds me at arm's length and looks me up and down. *Charming, and extremely feminine.* I feel her breath on my cheek as she bends forward to adjust the necklace.

The head waiter bows when he sees Aunt Naomi. *Professor*, he murmurs, *delighted to see you again, madam.* Aunt Naomi takes my elbow and although the man is turning to lead the way, she says, *Ricardo, this is my niece Louise.* Ricardo's small black eyes look me up and down and linger at my neckline. *Delighted to meet you, Miss.* He smiles in the direction of my coral necklace and turns away, flicking his napkin at a tablecloth. *He doesn't believe me*, Aunt Naomi whispers, and glances around the restaurant. *He thinks I'm being sly.* She smiles and glances around, smoothing her upper lip, until the wine comes. *Here's to Louise*, she says, raising her glass and leaning across the table to kiss me on the cheek. I drink the wine and feel my cheeks get hot.

The wine tastes better as I drink and Aunt Naomi keeps me amused with stories of uninhibited natives. From time to time I catch sight of myself in one of the wall-mirrors. The girl sipping from her glass and smiling at the woman opposite is definitely pretty. I'm conscious of being watched by people at tables and by Ricardo, standing with his napkin over his arm. A little flushed, but pretty. After dinner, Aunt Naomi orders two glasses of a sweet drink that tastes of oranges and makes my eyes water at the first sip. It glows through my chest and fumes rise into my head. There's still a little in the glass and it's some time since I've seen anything but the crumpled napkin in front of me, full of folds and shadows, when Aunt Naomi is behind me with a hand under my elbow helping me up, guiding me through the tables to the door. I don't remember the carpet being as thick as this, it must have some thick foamy layer underneath to give it this unsteady yielding feeling. Keeping my balance requires some concentration, someone should say something to them, this carpet could be dangerous. *Deadly carpet attacks birthday girl.* When Ricardo helps me on with my coat, and bows, I can't stop giggling long enough to say goodbye properly.

Aunt Naomi's shoulder is very comfortable as we drive home, and the orange lights of the highway make the journey interesting. I'm sure there's a way of telling exactly how fast we're going by the lights. The interval between the lights. Assuming they're all the same distance apart. And that we're not slowing down or speeding up. I try to work it out but I soon lose track of all thoughts.

My holiday by the sea is still less than half over, there are still weeks and weeks before I have to get on the slow train to take me back to the west, when Cheryl's brother Jeffrey asks me to a party. It will be my first party in the city, my first party without everyone's parents in the other room talking about the drought, my first proper grown-up party.

Aunt Naomi takes a moment before looking up from her piles of the **Voolalu Courier**. She's wearing her glasses today and looks stern. *That's grand, darling. Grand.* She pats a pile of clippings into tidiness. *Now this Jeffrey. I've met him, haven't I?* She peers at a clipping that says *Three Balls and a Pudding-Beater* in smudged headlines. *I'm sure he's a very worthy young man.* She pauses and I wait. *Your mother will have told you all about the birds and the bulls, I suppose.* She giggles and stops. *Hasn't she?* She shuffles through the piles of clippings and stops at a blurry photo which she stares at before quickly moving it to the bottom of the pile. *You've got to be terribly careful, darling. I'm sure Jeffrey is a very upright young man but I want you to promise me . . . don't let him tell you it's all right because everyone does it. It isn't and they don't.*

The yellow dress is my prettiest so I wear it for Jeffrey. He blushes and fingers his chin where a few pale hairs are sprouting and tells me I look terrific. At the party we sit down on the rolled-up rug and he tells me about his Ford. He's going to have to get new tappets but before that he's planning to get a Lukey muffler since that improves mpg and sounds better too, more sporty. He's very good at car noises and demonstrates the difference between his engine when it's well tuned and when the plugs are coked up. He sits on the rug holding the wheel in one hand, shifting gears with the other while his feet do a double-declutch dance on the floor and the acceleration makes his head jerk back. He shifts back down through the gears, the engine whining into second, and softly jerks to a stop. *We dance for a bit?*

On the floor he gathers me into his blue suit and steers me swiftly around the room, smiling vaguely over my shoulder and holding my hand out to the side like someone demonstrating life-saving. When they put a slow one on and turn off a few more lights, he lets my hand drop and holds me around the waist, humming into my hair. I yield against him and slide my hands along his padded shoulders. When he kisses me I feel his cheek, smooth, with only the odd hair, almost like mine.

We leave the party early and drive up the coast to a small beach between high dark cliffs, where he parks the car facing the breakers. When the engine stops, the sound of the surf is quite clear, sliding up glassily through the sand, sucking back out with an asthmatic rattle. We stare out through the windscreen at the pale lines of surf forming and dissolving until the windows steam up. *I can put the radio on if you like*, Jeffrey whispers, *but the surf's kind of nice.* He takes off his coat and puts it on the back seat. *Like you*, he says, and kisses me. His hands rub up and down my waist and we get very hot and moist as he sighs into my ear and squeezes my breasts through the yellow dress. *Nice*, he whispers. *The sporting model.* My clothes are tight and twisted but I enjoy his sighs and the way he kisses.

I'm searching in the bottom of my bag for the key when Aunt Naomi opens the door and leads the way into the kitchen. *I'm going to sound like a terrible old bore, Louise*, she says gravely, *but it's very late.* She opens a drawer, glances in, closes it again. *Long after twelve, darling.* She looks at me for the first time and watches my hand as it tries to smooth my hair. I'm spotlit under the glaring kitchen light and as she looks at me licking my swollen lips she rubs a finger over her own mouth. *You know, Louise, men are dreadful rapacious creatures.* She laughs. *You think I'm just being a gloomy widow I suppose but I know a thing or two about men.* She turns away to the sink, fills a glass of water and takes a sip. *They won't respect you, although they'll promise you the moon and stars.* She laughs again. *Naturally they'll become eloquent about love and so forth.* She takes another gulp of water and some spills down her chin. *But it's not just the little brown folk who are all after the one thing, Louise.* She rinses the glass under a stream of water so hard it splashes her dressing-gown and makes the vermilion cloth very bright. *All men are only thinking about one thing, Louise.* She puts the glass down on the sink so violently we both stare at it as if expecting the cracks to appear. *And I'm responsible for you, Louise, and cannot send you back with anything missing.* She leans back against the sink and smiles, flapping the wet lapel of her dressing-gown back and forth. *Your father has wanted an excuse to take a whip to me, ever since we were children.* She smiles again, showing a lot of teeth, and I smile back. There is a long silence in which she watches me closely. Finally she sighs. *Well, time for bed darling. But remember, they're obsessed with it.*

When I hurry through the chores on Saturday, eager to meet Jeffrey, I can't find one of my pairs of panties. I know I had seven pairs, but although I look everywhere, even in the bed where the flabby hot-water bottle is a nasty shock, the seventh pair is definitely missing. Aunt Naomi comes in as I'm hanging the others out, but I don't mention it to her.

Before she lets me go rollerskating with Jeffrey she reminds me that she is responsible for me and that I have to be careful. *There'll be some pretty unsavoury types hanging round the rink. Some men think it's a good joke to give a young innocent girl a shock.* She stares hard at me. I have no idea what she means and stare back. *They're sick, of course.*

As she's opening the front door for me to go out to the street where I can see the Ford, she holds my arm. *One more thing, darling, when you fall over on your skates there'll be people wanting to help you up, they'll be all over you like a rash. You tell Jeffrey to stay with you.* As I'm going down the path she calls out, *If you have a fight with him, phone me and I'll come and get you.* I wave and get into the car, and although she seems to have

62

more to say she stops herself and waves as we drive away.

Jeffrey is a good skater and speeds around the rink leaning slit-eyed into the curves, glancing over his shoulder as he accelerates with a roar to overtake some Sunday skater, finally bucking to a halt beside me at the rail. *You're pretty good on those*, he says. *How about a Coke?*

Under the huge old tree in the park outside the rink we lie looking up into the dark leaves and twisted branches. *Good for climbing in, these,* Jeffrey says. He rolls over towards me. *First rate for kissing under, too.* His hands slide around my waist and I feel my blouse coming untucked from my jeans. His hands move firmly, sliding up towards my breasts. Something lands on the ground near my face and we both jump. *Hell*, says Jeffrey, *they shitting on us up there or is it these seed things?* Still lying half over me, he laughs and I feel his stomach quiver. *Well, so much for the romantic under the trees lark,* he says, helping me up, still laughing. He doesn't let go of my hand as he says quickly, *listen you and me get on pretty well, you want to go round together for a while?*

Aunt Naomi continues her warnings. *If there's a pool at this party, Louise, and they want you to go swimming, don't. There are men who think it's amusing to take a girl's clothes away while she's in the water. You never know who might be there, or what they might be after.*

A second pair of panties seems to have disappeared. They're not in any of the places they should be, nor are they under the furniture in my room, behind the dresser, or in any dark corner of the laundry.

Aunt Naomi used to lock the bathroom door carefully, but she's more careless these days. I open the door of the silent bathroom and she's standing naked in the middle of the room, doing nothing unless perhaps looking at herself in the mirror. The house is getting smaller and smaller.

Louise, she says at lunchtime over the *Spaghetti Fantastico, I don't want to alarm you but I've just been reading about something I think you should know about. I know Voolalu seems a long way away, but men are the same everywhere. He was using some kind of pump to wash her out with hot soapy water. Terrible thing. Squirted it right up inside. She was white as a fish when they found her.* A morsel of spaghetti hangs from her chin and trembles at each word. As I watch, it falls off and lands on the table. She glances at me and dabs around her mouth with the napkin.

The salt sticks to my skin and the top of my bikini rubs grittily across my back. *You're getting a bit burnt*, Jeffrey says, smoothing my shoulder. *You want to take this off and put my shirt on?* Spiky grey bushes conceal us from the beach and in this little clearing the sand is hot underfoot and full of twigs. The breeze doesn't reach us here and the steady roar of the breakers is muted. Jeffrey undoes the bikini top and smears suntan oil across my shoulders. *How's that*, he says. *Better?* I close my eyes against the dazzle and feel his hands smoothing the oil further and further around towards my front. *These aren't burnt*, he whispers into my ear from behind, *but I don't see why they should miss out.* My nipples stand up between his fingers as he presses against me. The thin shrieks of kids splashing in the shallows come as if from miles away. A dog barks quickly twice and stops. Jeffrey helps me on with his shirt and kisses me quickly on the cheek. *We'll go up in flames here*, he says and laughs. *Let's find a cool drink somewhere.*

Aunt Naomi still waits up for me every night when I go out with Jeffrey. I creep in each time, hoping to make it up to my room without having to face her, but the hall light suddenly snaps on and she stands staring at me from the top landing with the vermilion dressing-gown wrapped tightly around her. For each step I take up the stairs she takes one down, talking about burning candles at both ends and giving myself away cheap. Since she never believes me when I tell her we don't do anything, I've stopped trying to convince her. She stands over me watching my damp mouth, stands right over me where she must get a good whiff of the sweaty hot smell. I try to back away but she follows me down from step to step, talking about the dangers of disease and how a young girl's life can be blighted forever by an early mistake.

When the third pair of panties disappears, the white ones I know were in the laundry basket, I decide that it's time to mention it to Aunt Naomi. When I tell her that three pairs of panties are missing, and ask her whether she's thrown them out, she looks up vaguely from her salad. *Well, Louise,* she begins, her lips shining with salad oil, *why don't you ask Jeffrey?* She crams a whole lettuce leaf into her mouth and stares at me with a frill of green poking out before chomping and swallowing. *Why ask me, Louise? I'd suggest you ask Jeffrey.*

That weekend, I look in all the places I looked before. The white ones are now under my bed. The pink frills are behind the socks in my top drawer, and the pale blue ones are in the laundry basket tangled with one of Aunt Naomi's pillowcases.

The letters are starting to draw me back home. Father's letters are full of the times of trains, and how to make the connection at Yarloo. Mother's are full of all the things I must bring home, the mace for the spice cakes, that special tea that can only be bought in the city. I seem to have become a stranger to little Evie, whose letters to me have become formal, to someone who has moved out of her world. She no longer shares news of Bluey's pups or the way the treehouse has been renovated, but writes stiffly, *Dear Louise, How are you? I hope you are well,* as if to an aunt or uncle who must be thanked nicely for a present.

I am sorry to lose you, Louise, says Aunt Naomi, and hugs me so that I see her earlobe with its tiny pearl at very close quarters. She has put on a great deal of *Chaleur* today, and rustles in a new silk dress. *I've enjoyed having you, and getting to know you, Louise.* We seem to be starting our farewells rather too early, because I have two more days here with Aunt Naomi, and a last date with Jeffrey, but she is hugging me as if this is the moment of lifelong farewell.

Looking forward to going home? Jeffrey asks as he unbuttons my shirt and unhooks the bra, fumbling a bit in the dark. *You sorry to leave?* His hands rub up my thighs under the skirt. *Tell you what, I'm going to miss you.* He sighs and sits back as if depressed. *It's going to be lonely with you gone.* I'm going to miss Jeffrey, too. He's staring out the window now, with his arms crossed and his hands squeezed under his armpits. The loose elastic on these old panties makes it easy to pull them off, and they look so shabby I feel like rolling down the window and tossing them into the bushes. Jeffrey is still staring out the window but when I drop them in his lap he looks around quickly. This is my last night, the last night that Aunt Naomi will be waiting in her vermilion for me to come home. Tonight, I want to stay out till dawn.

Slow Dissolve

My name's gone from the label by the bell. Now there's just a neatly-typed C.Stone. I wonder how she likes it on her own. I can hear her coming down the inside stairs. A nice smile now.

— Caroline!

— Mirrie!

— Nice to see you!

— It's been so long!

I feel that my smile shows too many teeth. So does hers. We stare at each other's mouths for a moment.

— I kept meaning . . .

— Nearly phoned you . . .

— Absolutely flat out . . .

— Tried to call you . . .

And here we are. There was nothing to say when we shared this flat, and there's still nothing to say.

— Hope my things haven't been in your way.

— No, no, plenty of room.

— Good good I kept meaning.

— Cup of tea?

— Lovely thanks.

The smell of the kitchen is the same as ever. The ghosts of a thousand sausages still hang in the air. Greasy fluff clings to the leg of the stove as it always did. The gap in the lino is full of the same black crumbs.

Caroline is straight out of the pages of the glossy magazines. What London's best-dressed secretaries are wearing.

— You're looking good Caroline.

— Oh thanks but I'm a mess my hair's terrible today.

She still talks in a whine like a broken motor. Her sharp little cat-face only cracks its varnish to smile when absolutely necessary.

— That's a great dress, I say.

— Oh this old thing. Just an old thing for work.

Her eyes flicker over my collection from the jumble sales.

— You're looking good too.

Making the tea, she moves around the kitchen slowly as if drugged. There's a slow walk to the cupboard for the sugarbowl and she lifts it down slowly from the shelf. There's another slow walk back to the table with the sugar and a long consideration about where to put it. She hovers it down as cautiously as the helicopter containing the Queen. It might be dangerous to interrupt this trance but if I don't speak I'll break into a high-pitched cackle.

— Going away this summer?

— I don't really know.

She takes a teabag out of the box.

— I went away last summer.

After frowning thought she takes out another teabag.

— I went to Bermuda.

— That must have been good.

She closes the box carefully, as if small creatures are seething inside.

— It was all right.

The box is finally safe back on the shelf.

— Did you go there with someone?

— Yes, oh yes I went there with a fellow I knew here, see, he asked me to go, only we had a fight and then he came back here but I didn't want to so I stayed there.

After this she seems exhausted.

— But it must have been good being in Bermuda? Even without him?

The silence has set like old yolk.

— It was all right. Sun and . . . beaches. Beaches and . . . swimming and all that. I got a good tan.

She inspects a patch of arm.

— Gone now.

She scratches with a fingernail at the vanished tan.

— I was really brown. But it faded.

— You didn't meet anyone else?

— Well you see everyone there was like in a couple. Every man was with a woman and there weren't any free men. And it was really expensive. Eating cost a lot and even a Coke was nearly a pound.

She stares bleakly round the room.

— See, if I'd of found a man he could've taken me out to dinner and bought me drinks and that and I could've stayed at his hotel and it wouldn't have cost me hardly anything, he could've taken me out to dinner every night. I couldn't afford to eat hardly by myself, but all the men were with women, they'd brought them with them, see.

She stares at me until I nod, then goes on.

— Anyway just before I had to leave I found a man and it was all right then. He was kind of old but all right. But I only had a few days of that and then I had to go back home. But the last few days were okay it didn't cost me anything and I could move out of my hotel and all that and he could buy me dinner.

The kettle makes a stifled screaming noise and after staring at it for a moment she pours the water into the mugs. When she puts the kettle back on the stove it keens softly to itself.

— What about your boyfriend, I ask. Still seeing him?

— You mean Pete, well he and I broke up. He had a lot of money you know, quite well off really. But he was very mean with it. Never took me anywhere nice or anything.

She stirs her tea as if she plans to wear through the bottom of the mug with the spoon.

— I mean I don't expect people to spend a lot of money on me all the time or anything. But when they've got it, it seems mean I think. He had a good job and all that.

She shifts in the chair and smooths the skirt over her knees.

— And there was another girl of course. I knew about her all along, it was all right by me. But she was just out for what she could get. Clothes and fancy meals. Jewellery even. Then she just dumped him, must have got all she wanted.

She licks the spoon and holds its curve against her cheek as if warming herself.

— Makes you think doesn't it. Like you should be out for what you can get. I was with him two years, two years I spent on him.

The spoon must be cold and she flips it across the room towards the sink, where it skitters along the enamel and disappears down the back. She watches as if expecting to see it crawl back up.

— Two years. Nearly three really. And then we broke up and I'm back where I started.

Her lips pucker towards the steaming tea and for a moment she looks like an old woman with her teeth out. She sighs.

— Everything's so dear. I've got to get my hair done once a week and that's going on ten pounds right there. Then clothes, they get dearer all the time, but you've got to look nice, otherwise . . .

She glances at me but doesn't finish the sentence.

— And after two years.

She runs a hand down her shin, closely inspecting it. It's a fine shin, but the sell-by date is moving up fast and the goods will soon start to look a little shabby. With a sputter and pop she squeezes cream out of a bottle and smooths it into her hands.

— Want to get your things?

These two shabby coats, the boots that need mending, and the boxes of tired paints were hardly worth coming back for. The suitcase bulges when everything's packed in. I'm leaving her the broken pith helmet and the eiderdown that leaks feathers. She must get cold alone here at night.

The living-room is full of a faint twittering from the television, and ghostly shadows of colours move about on the screen. Caroline sits unblinking, staring at a huge mouthing face.

— I asked someone to meet me here at six, mind if I wait?

— Of course, fine.

She shifts in the chair so her body is receptively turned to me as if for a chat but her attention is now fixed on three women pointing at a wet floor.

— So what are you up to these days Mirrie, she says. Still doing your drawings?

I remind myself that the only artist she knows by name is Leonardo da Vinski.

— Yes. Paintings actually.

— And what about . . . still by yourself?

She waits for my well-practised explanation of how much I like living on my own. Practice makes perfect, but it makes a nice change to surprise her.

— Actually there's a man I'm seeing quite a lot of.

Caroline sits forwards in her chair.

— That's wonderful, she whispers. Wonderful.

Her eyes retreat to the television. I'm afraid she might suddenly crack the varnish and start to cry.

— It may not last, of course, I say. Who can tell?

She glances at me sharply. I see she's thinking there's already trouble.

— I mean, we just get on well. That's all.

Her attention on me is so great that I can see her inspecting first my right eye, then my left, for the truth. Her eyes are devouring my face.

— But I never believe in looking into the future.

Caroline nods and I hear myself rushing on.

— Just enjoy the moment, that's what I always say.

Caroline switches the television off and turns her full attention on me. I feel myself smiling brightly.

— Known him long?

— Three months.

She nods like a housewife sniffing a dubious grapefruit.

— What's he do?

— He's a designer.

— How old is he?

— Thirty-five.

— Sounds good. Planning to get married?

— We don't see the point of marriage. We don't believe a piece of paper makes any difference.

She nods but her smile doesn't seem quite convinced.

— Anyway, I've got my work.

She glances at my clothes again.

— Wouldn't it be easier if you got married?

One of my fingernails has just broken and I have to stop myself tearing at it.

— We just don't think it's necessary.

She glances out the window at the darkening sky.

— He been married before?

— Well yes. But it was a long time ago. And she was a bitch.

Caroline is rubbing a hand over and over the same patch of her knee. She's stopped watching me. Somehow she's got the wrong idea of all this.

Finally, in a voice that's a pitch too high, she says:

— Well that's wonderful Mirrie, I'm sure you'll be really happy, I certainly hope it all works out for you.

She snaps on the television again and switches from channel to channel. At last the doorbell rings.

— That'll be Allan now.

She glances at her watch and I can't avoid hearing what I know she's going to say, although I hurry out of the room:

— Bit late isn't he?

I run down the stairs two at a time. When I open the door, there he'll be, my lovely man. I open the door and Allan is staring at me as if he wants to break my nose.

— You gave me the wrong fucking address.

I start to apologize and put my hand on his shoulder but he pushes past me up the stairs. Up in the living-room, Caroline has turned off the television and is standing with a welcoming hostess smile. Allan barely glances at her.

— These your things?

He's already picked up my bag and is waiting for me by the door. Caroline is smiling, and keeps smiling as Allan goes heavily down the stairs.

— He's a real strong silent type isn't he, she says and giggles. Real strong and silent.

We can hear Allan get into his car and slam the door. He starts the engine with a gnashing sound and revs up so hard that the whole house seems to shake. When he gives a blast on the horn, the living-room is filled with the blare. Caroline and I stand staring at each other, listening to the noise echoing until at last it fades away.

Meeting the Folks

François is very handsome although he giggles too much. His brown eyes bulge a little as he stares at me, and his fingers tremble as he talks. He's a brilliant physicist and he's only twenty-eight. He's spent the flirting years locked away in a dark room with his molecules, but he's making up for lost time now.

Cautiously, I rehearse the letters home. Hi everybody, guess what. I'm living with a good-looking Frenchman. The world's at his feet. He taught at Stanford and his English is perfect. He's every girl's dream come true.

When he asks me to meet his family my heart goes pitter-pat.

— You will meet my mother. I'm sure you'll like her.

He thinks, and adds:

— She has aristocratic blood. The château has been in her family for hundreds of years.

A château! What will I wear?

— She can be a little difficult, he says.

He smiles his fixed smile.

— If she doesn't like people she can be a little harsh. She is very highly strung. But she has a heart of gold.

I nod and try to look confident.

— I am the youngest son and the only one not married. I am her baby, you know? And she hopes I do not marry just yet.

He stares at me and says rather loudly:

— But I do what I want. Not what she wants.

He continues to stare at me and I feel the daydreams jostling in the wings. They make such a lovely couple. Two of the most adorable kids you can imagine and very clever of course.

— Does your family speak English?

— Not my father. My mother, yes, but she prefers not to. She thinks she does not speak very well so she prefers not.

I wish I'd been working at my French a bit harder.

The train takes a long while to get to the town near the château. Usually François talks about himself when we're alone together, or tells me about physics. Today, though, all the way down in the train he asks me about myself and my family.

— You have brothers and sisters?

— One of each.

— What does he do, your brother?

— He's a surveyor.

— And your sister?

— She's a teacher.

— Your father, what is his job?

— He's a doctor.

— Formidable! That will impress them.

He grins at me as if we've cooked up a good story.

— And your job, before you came to France, what was it again?

— I worked in films. A continuity-girl.

— Ah yes.

He stares at me consideringly.

— Perhaps it would be better not to mention that. In France, people who work in films are often . . . my mother might think . . . if she asks, of course don't hide it, but don't bring it up.

There's a long silence.

— We will have separate bedrooms in the château. My mother is a little old-fashioned. She would think you were . . . she would not approve. But you will like her, I'm sure. She is very cultured. She reads Proust all the time. You know, Marcel Proust the writer?

At the station an old man whom I take for a chauffeur greets us. This is François's father, and he seems to like my name.

— Villiers? Vous êtes Française?

— Non, je suis Australienne.

— Ah.

His welcoming smile fades and he drops my hand and turns to François. Without another glance at me they walk to the car talking, and I trail along behind. With perfunctory politeness I am ushered into the back seat, which smells powerfully of dog. I sit on a blanket covered with dog hairs and try not to think about fleas.

We stop at the village market for a little shopping and I wander among the smells of dead flesh and strong cheese. Whole pheasants hang by their feet from hooks, and hares with glassy eyes are lined up on marble slabs, their delicate mouths encrusted with blood. On one counter a whole pig lies in state, surrounded by small birds.

I stare at some unfamiliar-looking meat on the next counter and wonder what the smell is. The meat is very red, chopped in rough chunks like wood. The man behind the counter comes over to me.

— Vous voulez, Madame?

— Oh non, je regarde seulement.

He hears my accent and comes closer, spreading his red-stained hands on the counter.

— Vous aimez les chevaux?

He's grinning, showing rotten teeth.

— C'est du cheval?

— Bah oui, bien sûr, c'est du cheval. Très bon, très bon.

He's leering at me over the counter, picks up a lump of horse meat and shoves it almost into my face.

— Très bon, très bon.

I back away and he laughs.

It's a long drive to the château. François interrupts his conversation with his father long enough to say over his shoulder:

— There are no buses here, no buses at all. It is twenty kilometres to the château and the only way is by car.

He grins his fixed grin.

The château isn't actually a castle, but a big two-storeyed farmhouse set in misty fields.

A woman comes out of the house and throws her arms extravagantly around François — a rosy-cheeked old lady with a great bush of white hair, wearing down-at-heel slippers and a cardigan full of holes. I think this must be an old family retainer but it turns out to be Maman.

— Chéri, chéri!

She ruffles François's hair and kisses his face again and again. We're introduced. She shakes hands very fleetingly and says, looking at François,

— Mais tu m'as dit qu'elle est . . . Australienne ou . . . bah . . . quelque chose . . .

— Mais oui, je suis Australienne.

She stares at me with hostility.

— Mais vous avez un nom francais!

The kitchen is a vast gloomy cavern with a stone floor. As I go in, huge dogs emerge out of the shadows in the corners. Some stand and bark at me but one cringes up, wagging its tail. It's a relief to have something to do so I pet it while a commotion of French happens around me and Maman tweaks at François's clothes, runs her hands over his chest and waist, exclaiming how much weight he's lost. She glances over at me petting the dog, comes over and shouts into my face as if I'm deaf,

— C'est sale, ce chien-là. Sale, comprenez? Dirty, dirty.

— Il me semble très gentil . . .

— Phoo! C'est sale.

She turns away. François puts his arm around her waist and asks her how it is she looks younger all the time, like a young girl. Later he takes me to show me the house.

— It's better if you don't pet that dog, he says with his eternal smile. Maman doesn't like that dog, it belongs to my brother.

We sit down and eat lunch. Each item is loudly criticized by Maman, who demands why the men have bought such rubbish. They've bought the worst meat in the country. Why are they so stupid? François grins at me, laughs, pats Maman's hand. Finally Papa protests mildly:

— Mais c'est mangeable, n'est-ce pas?

Maman takes out of her mouth the piece of slimy meat she's been chewing and throws it ostentatiously to one of the dogs under the table. Chin thrust forward, she stares across the table at Papa who munches on without further comment. François giggles and looks at me.

I'd been worried about which fork to use and all that. I'd never eaten with anyone of Aristocratic Blood before. However as the meal progresses I see I needn't have worried. Papa reaches across the table for a piece of bread and butters it straight on the tablecloth. Maman watches him, then takes the whole loaf and rips a piece off. She chews it briefly, then takes it out of her mouth — bah! — and flings it across the table where it lands beside my glass.

No-one says anything to me so I sit and eat in silence. Maman's loud voice ricochets around the bare stone walls of the room in competition with the barking dogs, who are fighting over the scraps which everyone has tipped off their plates onto the floor.

After lunch I rehearse my best French and offer to help Maman wash up. She stares at me as if I'm speaking Swahili and says to François:

— Qu'est-ce qu'elle dit?

François translates. She shrugs impatiently and mutters something I can't catch, then looks at him and laughs. He laughs too, and glances quickly at me. I look out the window.

In the next room is a huge grand piano. François sits down at this and plays something very hard with great skill. Then he says:

— I will let you try to guess this next one. See if you can.

I listen hard.

— Satie, isn't it?

His face falls.

— You knew it already.

— No, I guessed.

— A lucky guess! We'll have to try again.

We hear Maman in the next room, apparently moving furniture.

— Maman never learnt to play, but she is very musical, François says. He starts playing again, but Maman yells to him, and grinning at me over his shoulder, he goes in to her. For the next fifteen minutes everyone within a range of about a mile must hear Maman telling François that there is no room for the Australian to stay here. She finishes by bellowing:

— Where is she going to sleep?

François murmurs that I can have his room and he will sleep in the spare room but Maman is enraged by this.

— Why should you sleep with the boxes, she yells. There aren't enough sheets and she'll use all the hot water.

I try to believe that Maman doesn't know I understand French.

Later, he and Maman and I walk down to the next farm to buy a chicken. I trail along behind while they walk ahead, arm-in-arm, discussing local scandals, and try to concentrate on how beautiful the countryside is. The road curves down between hedges and a twittering flight of birds sweeps through the pale sky. François turns back.

— This is a French Oak, he says, pointing. You don't have these in Australia.

— No, we have other kinds of trees there.

At the farm I'm introduced by Maman simply as "L'Australienne". The farm women are very polite and ask me my name. Before I can answer, Maman says loudly that I don't speak French. She adds that François always brings foreigners here who don't speak French. Hoping to clear up this misconception, I tell them that in fact I do understand French, although I don't speak it terribly well. François's smile vanishes and he darts a distraught look at me. As we go in he whispers that I must not say anything to upset Maman.

Maman's voice fills this house as it fills her own. She talks on and on about the quality of meat while the farm women agree mildly. At one stage Maman glances at me and says very loudly:

— In Australia they eat nothing but sheep. Rien que mouton.

Her saliva lands on my face.

On the way back François lets Maman wander ahead and says to me in a low voice:

— It seems to be all right for a first meeting. You behaved very well.

Back at the house he brings out two chairs onto the terrace. Maman immediately appears from within and sits in one. There's a pause. François brings out another and the three of us sit admiring the misty fields, which are becoming less beautiful for me from moment to moment. François appears to be nodding off. Maman has a small smile on her face.

Finally he comes back to life and asks me if I'd like a cup of tea. I imagine a cosy pot for two in the kitchen and at last a few minutes alone together. But he bends over Maman and says:

— Maman, ma chérie, ma plus aimable Maman, mon amour, veux-tu du thé?

Maman sticks out her bottom lip.

— Non. Veux pas.

I'm pleased to hear this, but just as he's leaving for the kitchen she changes her mind, beaming at us like a sweet old dear. So tea is taken in the squalid formality of the dining room, where Maman issues a whole new series of complaints — about the tea, about the china François has chosen to use, about the brioche bought in the morning. Speaking very clearly, and loudly enough to rattle the cups in the next room, she asks:

— Are there many kangaroos in Australia?

— Yes, there are a great many, I say.

François watches me anxiously.

— They are grotesque animals, Maman asserts.

— Yes, they are rather odd.

— Monstrosities, she shrieks. The ugliest animals in the world!

She stares at me. Being careful to get it right, I say:

— Yes, they are a little peculiar, but they are unique to Australia.

Across the table I see François lean back out of Maman's range of vision and shake his head and frown at me.

— And the Aborigines, Maman continues. They are not really human at all. They are monkeys. Grotesque. God was joking when he made them. And you, Mademoiselle, do you have any Aboriginal blood?

— No, Madame, not as far as I know.

Maman leans back picking her teeth with her fingernail. I think with relief that she's come to the end of what she knows about Australia.

— But the coral, she says at last magnanimously. The coral there is quite good. I have a coral necklace which is not too bad. It's a kind of rock which occurs underwater. It can be quite pretty.

— I think it's a kind of small animal, like insects, they build it gradually over the years . . .

She stares at me with contempt.

— It's a rock, she says and stands up. Well, François, are you going to clear this mess?

François and I go back to the terrace. Papa, who has been

83

silent throughout tea, appears with a wheelbarrow and begins to trundle loads of gravel from a big heap onto the path. After each load he spreads it with a rake until it's perfectly even. Then he goes for another barrowload of gravel. He moves very slowly, looking dignified and aloof even when down on all fours on the path removing weeds. I ask François if he plans to spread gravel on all the paths.

— Oh yes, he always does this. By the time he finishes at the back, the gravel is washed away at the front again.

He shrugs and says:

— He does this now he is retired.

François decides to play some more Chopin. I sit at the end of the piano, an obediently admiring audience. Maman is constantly in and out of the room, measuring the sweater she is knitting him, asking what he wants for dinner, smoothing his hair, nagging about getting it cut. François protests:

— But Maman, doesn't it make me look distinguished?

She pretends to slap him and he catches her wrist and kisses her hand. She smiles down at him and they both glance over at me.

Dinner is no better than the other meals.

— Are you a good cook, Mademoiselle? Maman shouts, making mixing and eating gestures at me.

François winks across the table at me and says quickly:

— Oh yes, she's a superb cook. When we're married, she'll do all the cooking.

Maman stares first at me, then at François, who says:

— We plan to have a big family, Maman, so you'll have lots of grandchildren.

Even Papa is staring at François now, a mouthful of meat poised on his fork. François winks at me. Maman looks very old as she stares down at her plate. Suddenly she looks up and slaps him playfully.

— You love to tease!

But she glances anxiously at me. François smiles at the tablecloth in a non-committal way. She stares at his profile and there's a long silence until she turns to me.

— Do you still have your parents, Mademoiselle?

— Yes, they're both alive.

— Oh là!

She gives me a pantomine of astonishment before saying very clearly:

— They must be terribly old.

— Well, they are about your age, Madame.

She snorts and tears off a great chunk of bread, then hurls it clear across the table, where one of the dogs leaps up and catches it in his jaws.

After dinner everyone disappears and I stand in the middle of the piano room and wonder what to do. Maman has taken François off somewhere and Papa has vanished. Finally I sit down at the piano and start to play but within seconds François appears and puts his hands over mine on the keys.

— You will disturb Maman.

He disappears again without giving me any indication of what to do. When he next appears, nearly an hour later, I tell him I want to have a bath and go to bed and he leaps at the idea, taking me upstairs at once and demonstrating how to turn the taps on and off for the bath.

Later, in bed, I hear the rest of the family go to their rooms. The conjugal bedroom is directly below mine and I hear through the floorboards Maman continuing to exclaim and shout, though I can't hear the words. At last all is quiet.

The door opens, very slowly, and François tiptoes in. With a huge signalling for silence he comes to the bed and whispers:

— Get down on the floor.

I do so and he makes love, holding me down so I can't move. Each time I take a breath he puts his hand over my mouth.

— Shhh. Shhh.

One of my legs becomes cramped and I move it slowly. He holds me down even tighter.

— Sssssh!

As soon as he finishes, he stands up, pulls his pyjamas back on and grins down at me.

— The bed is very noisy, he whispers. And Maman is right underneath.

I feel weak from the rigours of the day and my leg is still cramped. I lie and stare up at him but I can't be bothered to smile back. Suddenly he jumps on the bed and bounces up and down vigorously. The bed sets up a loud rhythmic rattle and squeak.

— Very noisy, he whispers. He lies still, seems to wait.

Underneath, Maman gives one short, wide-awake cough. We hear it very clearly in the quiet. François stares at me with wide eyes and starts to laugh silently, covering his mouth with his hand, making the bed shake. When I stand up I see that he's crying with laughter and biting his fist to keep it in. I leave him there and spend a long time sitting in the bathroom staring at the floor. When I come back to the bedroom, François has gone and the house is silent.

Junction

Will the girl with brown hair on the 4:15 from Gayton last Thursday who smiled at the man on the platform please call Doug on 467 3241.

He stays in all day all night. He leaves his door ajar to listen for the phone. He cleans his teeth very quietly and he doesn't play the radio.

The haggle-faced old onion of a woman who runs the rooming house thinks he's a good tenant but he makes a lot of noise these days leaping up the stairs tripping every time on the cracked lino to be the first to get to the phone.

— Yes yes yes hello hello.

— Oh. I'll see if he's in.

It's never for him. He puts off going to the toilet she might phone. He doesn't linger there over *Playboy* like he used to ignoring the rattling door handle. The landlady thinks it's a good sign maybe he's looking for a job at last.

He's in there and the phone rings. He leaps up grabs for the chain in a frenzy misses and gets the light-string instead, flails in the dark for the chain scrabbles at the lock and leaps up the stairs holding his pants up with one hand one shoe comes off when he trips on the lino but he's first to the phone.

— Hello hello yes yes yes

— No this is 467 3241 that's okay bye.

His pants are slipping down and the landlady's staring at him through her aura of old cooking fat.

— Expecting a call are you?

— No yes not really sort of

He makes it back to his room and sits on the side of the bed feeling constipated. The light struggling in through his window lies listlessly on the gritty mat. The corners of the room are very square and the walls stand drearily on guard.

It's three o'clock so he starts to get dressed. He wears the same clothes every day when he goes to meet the 4:15 from Gayton otherwise she won't remember him. He shaves very carefully avoiding the pimples and cuts himself only once on the rusty blade. The cold water makes his face blue but he wets his hair and combs it flat. Then he thinks that makes him look too young so he rubs it dry and tries to make it look casual.

Each day he buys a bunch of violets from the ancient woman who sits like a toad among her flowers.

Something told me I'd see you today so I bought these.

Or perhaps:

I bought these they go with your eyes.

But what if her eyes are brown?

They should be forget-me-nots because I remembered you.

He races up and down the train looking in every carriage it only stops for seven minutes. He stumbles along tripping over the straw baskets and grey-faced dribble-nosed kids in the corridor and when he gets to the end of the train and jumps off, the violets are wilted and greasy but he doesn't want to throw them away they remind him of her so he stuffs them in his pocket.

He tries to look indifferent as he passes the toadwoman

on the way out but she winks evilly at him and cackles through her gums and he hears the 4:15 pulling away from the station.

By the fourth day the ticket collector is grinning as he takes the platform ticket and on the fifth day as he takes the ticket he says something to the ex-jockey who sells papers and they both guffaw.

Will the girl on the 4:15 from Gayton last Thursday with short brown hair wearing a red raincoat who smiled at the man on the platform call Doug on 467 3241 I think I love you.

In his room he boils an egg and eats it with revulsion he wishes he knew how to cook. Then he sits and burps and stares at the spatters on the tiles behind the cooker and waits. The pus-coloured walls are closing in so he goes for a walk looking carefully at every girl he passes it might be her it might be her.

None of them is her.

He walks slowly back through the old milk cartons and crumbled dog turds and hears the phone ringing inside the house. Lunging his hand in for the keys he rips his pocket drops the keys grabs them they slip his hands are sweaty he rams the key at the lock it won't go in he's using the wrong key he drops them again but snatches them up before they hit the ground jabs the key into the lock can't remember which way to turn it finally gets the door open his nose is running his ears are burning he pounds up the stairs and the phone stops ringing.

He wants to throw his head back and bay savagely at the moon but there's only peeling paint above his head and the landlady in curlers and clotted dressing-gown is standing at the foot of the stairs looking up.

— She'll phone again love, nice boy like you, she says with heavy irony.

He worries that he'll miss her so next day he goes down the train twice, once in each direction, to make sure. The flatfaced old women growing out of the seats are staring at him now and he's panting and stumbling and knocking kids out of his way as he gallops up and down the corridor. An old woman with a wrinkled face like the top of a custard mutters crossly at him. A kid cries and rams its knuckle into its eye the man hit me WAAAAAAAAAAAAAH. The guard comes up.

— Wotcha doin' mister lookin' for someone?

— Yeah that's right.

His eyes are flickering round what if she goes past while this moron's blocking the view.

— Yeah yeah certainly no won't do it again, okay, he mumbles and sidles past while the guard stares suspiciously. She's not on the train.

Next day he gets to the station at three and the toad-woman tells him: You're early love, and makes a noise like a dog barking. He catches a train to the next station back up the line so he can get on the 4:15 from Gayton there. That way there'll be plenty of time to look for her. On the way they pass the earlier train from Gayton. He strains to separate the blur of carriages and there's a flash of red my god his heart leaps: there she is I've missed her. He searches the 4:15 but without hope.

The ticket collector suggests he get a season ticket for the platform. Ha ha.

He dreams of her all night and wakes panting as she eludes him again. He wakes with his hand clutching the corner of her raincoat which turns before his eyes into the corner of the sheet. Wakes breathless and heart thudding after running after her, she's on the back platform of a train which always goes just a little too fast and he keeps stumbling over his pants which have fallen around his ankles. The toadwoman cackles and her face withers like a piece of newspaper about to burst into flames. He sees a red coat on the other side of a crumbling mountain of straw baskets which he desperately climbs to get to her they fall on top of him his feet become wedged in them he's almost on top of them the train jerks into movement and he falls awake sobbing.

He sees her everywhere. Dashes after women in the street but they're never her. He spends a fortune in hamburgers he leaves to harden when he rushes out to chase a red raincoat across the road. Nearly gets arrested: Whereja think ya goin' gotta pay ya know. He nearly gets killed: Why doncha look where ya goin' dummie. Kindly old men creak after him: Hey sonny sonny you forgot your newspaper.

There's a wet spell and red raincoats are everywhere. He's getting a lot of exercise and not much to eat. When he can't sleep he writes poetry.

> Red is the colour of my true love's coat,
> Brown is her hair and short.
> My love's like a small brown bird
> That never will be caught.

This he copies neatly into a special book with a red cover. He buys a red raincoat and hangs it at the foot of his bed and puts the violets in the pockets. He buys a brown wig and the woman winks slyly as he chooses it: Yes dearie that looks real nice on you you take my word for it. He keeps it on his pillow at night but his landlady finds it and lingers in the hall outside talking loudly about deviants.

He searches the 4:15 for the last time. He comes home.

He puts the wig on, puts the raincoat on and takes his pants off. He stands in front of the mirror staring at himself with his hand moving faster and faster in the rubbery smell of sweaty raincoat, tears rolling down his face until at last he groans and doubles over holding himself as if shot.

Will the girl with blond hair and blue ribbons waiting for a 63 bus Friday at noon please call Doug on 467 3241.

Having a Wonderful Time

There's something about travel that brings on generalizations about the meaning of life. Maybe that's why we do it. Every departure's like a brushing acquaintance with death: getting in practice.

Even at the bus station in Earl's Court my bed-sitter seems like an abstraction on another planet. Desk here chair there bed here. All the flimsy brown-paper makeshifts fall away and leave us shivering. Standing by our bags waiting for the bus we eye each other. At the end of the next three days some of these strangers will have become people, and who knows what might happen. It could be anything. Three days on a bus is not an attractive prospect but think of it this way it will be an adventure. Think of it like that.

Yes John it will be like that. An adventure. Being your second-best woman has not been an adventure. Being your Wednesday woman has only been fun on Wednesdays.

You know what your trouble is you're too introspective you know that? Snap out of yourself a bit. Travel. Do you the world of good.

There are a lot of Australians going to Athens, like

migratory birds. That girl over there with the flat face looks Australian. That low shining forehead, that sharp chin, that lipless slit of mouth. Her huge breasts are contained in a well-upholstered bra like a comfortable armchair. The points of her nipples are grubby where they've brushed against things.

Is it because I'm one of them that I have to sneer?

That man in the check shirt looks American. His enormous hiking boots have curved up at the toes and look like cobblestones on the ends of his legs. Great arms like hams, he's a real meat-eater. Beside him, a dark dapper little man sits neatly on a neat pack with not a loose strap anywhere, as tidy as a block of butter. He sits and methodically eats a sandwich and makes something in me shrivel.

That what you mean, getting out of myself? Seeing how the other half lives?

I've got to get a window seat. Three days and two nights falling out into the aisle will not be an adventure. Or if it is, in my generosity I'll let some other poor bugger have the pleasure. Get the elbows in there. Pretend you don't see them thinking She jumped the queue the bitch. A foot on the bottom step and the bag casually held at the side blocking any bright ideas from the crowd behind me. Okay now. In we go quick. Not too far back it bounces. Not over the axle where the floor runs in a ridge. This one will do nicely thanks. Now sit back and look innocent.

The man who sits beside me is like a blond Greek god. I imagine his pectorals erect launching a javelin. An adventure! We exchange hellos. We establish that we are both going to Athens. We establish that he is Greek, but studies in England.

— I study to be a pilot.

— That must be interesting.

— It is all right.

We're still in dreary Penge or somewhere but the driver is giving us a taste of Greece. The beginning of our journey coils around and swallows its tail and suburban London stands amazed, blank windows exclaiming an empty O as the shimmering thump of bouzouki music fills the bus.

— What is your name, I ask.

— Costas. Means King, he explains with a modest smirk.

I think of my collection of conversation stoppers. I knew someone once who lived in that street. I bought this suit five years ago for ten pounds.

— I have a friend who learnt to fly, I say.

That's not much good. I knew a man once who lived in that street. I try again:

— He had to learn Morse Code, do you learn that too?

Costas leans in impatiently.

— What?

— Morse Code.

I enunciate so clearly that in a moment of sudden silence the whole bus hears.

— Moose . . . ?

— No, Morse, you know, dot dot dash dash. With a little machine . . .

I mime the flickering wrist of a Morse operator. Costas watches stonily. Dot dot dot dash dash dash dot dot dot. Help I am sinking. Mayday.

Costas calls out in Greek and the driver turns up the volume of the bouzouki.

Is it really such a good thing to have quite that number of St Marys and St Christophers and St Whoever-Elses and rosary beads and bunches of good-luck garlic dancing against the front window of the bus? And that large efficient-looking clock trying to tell us it's one o'clock at half-past nine? Never mind, it's got to be right twice a day. And we can eat the garlic if we get marooned. We going anywhere near Transylvania?

Here I am. Travelling. Broadens the mind. Maybe I should be taking notes. Look at these houses. Like boxes. Not very original. The hedges. What would I say about the hedges? Very neighbourly the way that one is clipped like a poodle to exactly the point where it becomes the next-door hedge and then sprouts wildly. Not an inch more. A man is trimming with an electric hedge-clipper, standing back to admire before he hovers in to take off one last errant leaf. Well another day gone, anyway. Yairs spent the weekend in the garden.

On the boat across the Channel there's a sudden sense of being in the team. You're on the bus too aren't you, whispers the girl with the grubby nipples, Do you know what we're supposed to do? A gangling man in front has reached the tea counter and clutches the top of his head with his arm as he says,

— Aaaaaah, cn Oi ev two cips a coffee?

When we get off the boat there's a long unexplained Greek wait. I decide with profundity that waiting bears the same relation to travelling as matter does to anti-matter and fight the suspicion that the bus has left without us. Another Australian girl with a face like Head Nurse, wearing a singlet and tight shorts, follows me around the wharf.

— Then I got the boat to Cairo, only twenty-seven pounds. Then, there was this train down to Khartoum and from there I got the plane to Algiers. Really dirty. The toilets, well you wouldn't credit it.

On the wharf where we all stand hopelessly waiting, a group of Americans is also waiting to be saved from the empty glare of this hazy non-place. They stand in a circle talking to each other with their bright backpacks ringing them around, like colourful humped birds. Everyone's on the move. Keep looking keep looking. What are you after anyway says John. You wanta learn to relax.

I'd like to convince myself that my failures can be left behind across this stretch of greasy undulating water. I can start again! Come to Sunny Greece discover a New You.

France is a blue smog haze. Great tangles of pipes and tanks twisting solidly up into the non-sky, huge blank buildings the colour of nothing as we speed past. Tall dumb chimneys forever point the way: up there it's up there. Neat triangular heaps of slag rise out of the mist, monumental, lingering. As one is left behind, fading into distance, another takes its place. Or is it the same one fooling us?

Before John there was Jim. My wife doesn't understand me. Before Jim there was Jerry. Baby you're dynamite, see you round. Before Jerry there was Jack. You're a million dollars baby but don't call me at home.

Each pyramid of slag marches out of the distance promisingly and sweeps past with the same empty symmetry as the others. The world is so leached of colour that an orange hoarding in the fields is like a shout. A bright blue silo booms, and a shiny red tractor is a yelp.

— Then I got the plane to Madrid and from there I got the morning train to Lisbon. That would have been the twenty-eighth of July, no I beg your pardon the twenty-ninth. Then I got a bus to this little place called Ortago, quite nice but the toilets were that smelly. Then must have been the second of August I took the plane from Lisbon to Barcelona.

Electricity pylons walk solidly off into the haze, striding with long praying-mantis legs, unswerving. Some march along with a bundle held aloft on each hand, others like amputees hold only one set of wires. The power must get through.

It's starting to get warm in here. Around me a great rustling of paper bags has begun and in a moment the air is full of orange peel and cheese sandwich. I root in my own bag and bring out an apple. On second thoughts I snap out of myself and get a bit involved and offer another one to Costas. He takes it with hardly a glance. Gotta learn to give a little, give and take, that's what it's all about.

In front of me two more Australian girls with tight shirts and closed smug faces are really getting organized. Long loaves of pre-buttered bread. Salami. Tomatoes and the right kind of knife, no squelchy mess here oh no, these girls didn't come down in the last shower. Even salt, in a shaker, with a special lid so it doesn't spill. Paper napkins, I don't believe it. They sit munching while around me others spill biscuits out of burst paper bags, dribble oranges on their legs, and spray exploding drink cans into the back of my neck.

— Gee sorry.

The two young men behind are looking apprehensive and also trying not to snicker.

— That's okay.

They are polite and watch each other's mouth as they speak, watch mine as I speak, although they are not lip-reading deaf-mutes. They are a pair of nice boys, off to Athos, they tell me, to check out the monasteries. No women are allowed anywhere on the peninsula of Athos, they inform me, not even female animals. They cannot stop themselves snickering at this. Boats containing women are forbidden to come closer than half a mile to the shore. It's almost enough to give you the feeling women might have something after all. Wonder if they strip you off at the entrance to make sure. And what is it they really get up to in there? Little leather lap-laps like the Masons maybe, standing displaying their paraphernalia at cock-crow.

Afternoon wears on. Are we still in France? Belgium? Luxembourg?

The drama of a frontier: this is Germany. Everyone's important with their passports. Head Nurse with her trembling thighs in shorts shows me her visas. Look I've been here and here and here and the toilets were that smelly. Travel broadens the bum.

Night falls and the Australians in front produce air-cushions and blow them up. No doubt about these Aussies they've got themselves organized. How come I didn't turn out like that? A blanket over the knees, snug as a bug in a rug.

Hey what kind of bitch are you? Where's your sense of adventure? Your joy in the rich pageant of multifaceted humanity? The glowing tapestry woven with a thousand gleaming strands which is Life? Where were you when the smiles were handed out? Huh?

Costas twitches and slumps beside me, trying to sleep. Bugger him if I'm going to offer my seat.

At some dead time of the night we stop for petrol and pisses. Grubby-Tits is clutching herself between the legs, Ooooo I've gotta go. We line up in the toilet staring at our reflections in a leprous mirror, listening to each other. Unbuckle unbutton unzip. Aaaaah.

Everybody has tried the coffee machine beside the bus. English money doesn't work, nor does French. No-one has any German money. When everyone has tried and gone away, the bug twins come and produce a little bag marked *Foreign Money*. They stand sipping coffee while around them we all blink blearily. Sorry, that was all we had, they say. But here have a sip.

In the morning when we wake we're twisting laboriously through mountains. The Andes? The Alps? The Himalayas? It's raining. Drops streak sadly down my window and on the windscreen huge wipers bend gracefully into each other like dancers. De de de de DAH, de DAH, de DAH.

Around a bend in the road a deep valley spears off into mist, a twisting vee weaving between interlocked spurs. Above us the ridges claw the dull sky with serrated edges like a child's scribble. The bus is very silent.

As the valleys flatten out and the rain stops, the bus comes to life. The bug twins squash the air out of their cushions with a rude noise. They tuck the blanket beneath housewives' double chins and fold it carefully. Then they produce little bottles and clean — cleanse, rather — their faces, and settle back without any expectation of surprise for another day. Oh yairs we did Europe.

The last night with John, before goodbye forever, he said as we got into bed: I've decided I like the outside of the bed best. Then he told me the one about the condemned man being led to the gallows. Someone offers him brandy. Oh yes he says eagerly. Never tried it before, maybe I'll like it.

Horses and mountains and chickens and cows pass. I discover that by rubbing a finger on my teeth I can make an internal squeaking noise. Different pitches on different teeth, doh ray me. Locked in solitary confinement, a person could become a virtuoso on teeth. Get out of prison and start an orchestra. Great to watch but maybe a little hard to hear. You could have heard a tooth squeak.

Boredom's like that. Someone should start a brain bank for when you get tired of your own. Better than shuffling through the tired old pack of Europe.

When we stop again we hover near the bus like nervous

children afraid of being left behind. We've lost track now, no-one knows for sure what country we're in.

— So anyway then I got the plane to Rome and I went to Florence on the train. Nearly missed it, they've got another name for it. Really dirty train with all these peasants stinking of that garlic. Rude and ignorant. Not a word of English between the lot of them. Don't talk to me about Italy.

Head Nurse has a voice of such authority it threatens to burst her singlet but boy she's been everywhere. You name it, she's been there. And the toilets were smelly and the peasants were rude and ignorant. She says to Grubby-Tits, who's staring open-mouthed and impressed:

— Why'ncha sit next to me, we'll have a real good chin-wag.

Her chin is muscular, the fittest chin in the world, the Mr Universe of chins, from so much wagging.

A leathery peasant shuffles past staring at her. His toothless face is like a squashed shoe.

— Wotcha staring at, dumb-bell, she says loudly.

These mountains are rather nice. Silhouetted pine trees walking up their spines — like black paper cut with pinking shears and pasted on to a white sky. Orange autumn trees among the dark pines give a stippled effect like trout. The hills hold blue shadows in their laps, their peaks crisp in the sun. Pines as straight as pencils spear up the slopes. We speed through a village while a cracked bell tolls clang clang clang. There's a church of soft ochrous plaster painted all over with small pink crosses. The ambitious sign on the Hotel Moderna is almost too faded to read.

We stop and the man with the neat pack gets out, waves tidily and walks off. There's a man who knows where he's going. Quick as a flash Costas takes the window seat he's left empty.

The border into Yugoslavia seems all guns and stubbly big-jowled faces and those peaked caps that South American dictators wear. The border guards swagger through the bus rudely going through everyone's plastic bags full of orange-peel and embarrassing crusts. Costas gives them a couple of packets of cigarettes and they leave him alone. No flies on this boy. They thumb laboriously through our passports while we sit waiting and sweating. I promise I'm not a terrorist. Honest, I've never seen a drug in my life.

We trundle off into dusk. Slavic faces stare sternly at us from doorways where kerosene lamps hang, and in the fields wooden carts creak along behind horses. A late worker in a field trudges behind his horse, ploughing, bored, dreaming of soup.

In the early morning we pass Mount Olympus and I remember that this is my adventure. We're nearly there. The mountains sprawl over the plain like vast sleeping hounds lying with their paws towards a fire. The gods are up there on that lumpy mountain, and somewhere not far away is the navel of the world. How feeble and faulty those gods are: Zeus with giant godly prick raised at some poor wee thing in the woods. Maybe I should turn into a tree.

Athens. Hieroglyphics instead of street signs. Not a word of English between the lot of them. My feet are huge as I hobble off the bus. Grubby-Tits is moaning:

— Ooooooh, me feet are that swelled up.

Head Nurse strides away, map in hand, to the Youth Hostel. Then I got the bus down to Greece, nice bunch of people, gave them a few tips about where to go and that.

I'm alone. I think I'll like Athens. The pavements are made of marble but everything smells of shit.

Time to drop a card to John. Make it nice now.

Dear John, had a great trip down on the bus. A nice bunch of people. Got chatting to a few Australians and a handsome Greek too. Saw lots of Europe. You were right, I needed an adventure. See you round, Louise.

Refractions

Once a year, for a week, the Harbour is surprised by a deep red stain throughout its waters. For a week, the tides that jostle the hairy pilings move sullenly as if conscious of some shame, and the seagulls shift from one foot to the other and inspect their underwings at length, waiting out this time when the water is dark and opaque and fishing is impossible.

One drop at a time, the dark red water is as clear as ever. The spray that flies off the tips of Louise's oars and lands on the seat of the dinghy dries without a stain, and the oars themselves, bone-white from the years, do not emerge dripping red. From time to time, as she pulls slowly around the headland, Louise feels a jellyfish cling to the oar for a moment before falling back sluggishly into the water. No matter how many loads of sticky jelly she tosses up onto her ragged lawn, no matter what masses of flies gather and crawl over the melting heap, and no matter how many black trails of ants lead away from it into the bushes, it is impossible to get rid of all these flaccid domes from the Harbour during its season of red water. She slices down hard with the oars and can imagine jelly severed by the blade and translucent shreds of flesh floating in the wake. The jellyfish have arrived with the red stain and will disappear with it, but for this week they drift through the Harbour, the lace-like frill around their edges undulating as they move slowly along the currents.

In the small park at the entrance of the bay, children scramble up and down the sea-wall, dislodging periwinkles and squealing at the sliminess of a captured jellyfish. On a still afternoon such as this, when each oar cuts through a palpable film on the water, the children and their dogs sound the same at a distance. Dogs nose at the lovers lying under the trees, and utter short boasting cries as they leap to fetch a stick thrown into the water. Men alone sit on benches, with ample room beside them for three or four companions, and watch closely as the lovers stand up and the woman plucks her damp dress from the back of her thighs. The children hurl their slimy handfuls at each other and shriek. When a jellyfish lands wetly on the ground, blades of grass and leaves cling to its surface and after a short time the first exploratory ant begins to investigate the frill.

Feeling the oar bite deeply into the water, Louise swings the boat sharply to enter the long narrow bay. On the bank a wet dog with streaming stringy hair runs along the edge of the sea-wall, pursuing the boat, barking and scrabbling at the edge of the rocks as if looking for a path across the water. It follows her as far as the fence where the park ends and a shapeless patch of scrubby waste ground has resisted civilization. There the dog cocks its leg at the palings and delivers itself of a brief glittering stream. Louise can remember when the whole headland was covered with this dull scrub. In those days she rowed to the point and went ashore to explore with a water-bottle hanging from her belt and a long whippy stick for the snakes. Now, years later, there are no longer any snakes, but once or twice every summer, a child will scream suddenly from the bushes and limp home crying, one hand on the shoulder of a supporting friend and the other holding the curved shard of dark beer-glass.

The man rises from the bushes as smoothly and silently as a periscope and stands half-hidden behind branches. She sees his head turn slowly as his attention is drawn towards the park, where two children, their sex indeterminate at this distance, are trying to prevent the dog from rolling on its back near the fence. They tug at its collar and thin shrieks carry across the water, but Louise sees the dog's paws in the air as it writhes in ecstasy on something beside the fence. As Louise rests on her oars she sees the children swing themselves around the end of the fence where it drops off at the edge of the sea-wall, and crouch on the other side of it, waiting for the dog to have had enough and wonder where they have gone. They crouch behind the fence and Louise remembers how it feels to be panting and giggling and trying not to make a sound, squatting, feeling a dry grass stem tickling the back of a bare leg and an ant running across a foot, peering through a crack in the fence.

A little way along from where they take turns at pressing their noses to the crack, Louise sees a glint as the man raises his hand to the front of his shirt and his shiny watchband catches the sunlight. His head swivels on his neck so that he is now staring straight at Louise across the short distance of water that separates them. As he undoes the last button of the shirt, he glances again towards where the children crouch, and hesitates before pulling the shirt off and dropping it beside him. Something gold on his chest glitters as he runs his hands over the muscles.

The dog is shaking itself vigorously. Louise sees debris fly off its body like dust off a mop twirled from a window, and sees the children shift in anticipation behind the fence, one now crowding on top of the other so they can both look through the crack at once. The dog noses along the ground in a loose circle, raises its head to sniff, and lollops to the fence to stand against it, tail waving like a ragged banner, so that it must be eyeball-to-eyeball with the children. Louise hears excited shrilling as they back away from the fence and begin to pick their way through the bushes to hide where the dog cannot see them. Louise remembers the brittle grey quality of the sunlight in the mazes of the scrubby bushes, the sandy soil underfoot full of twigs and small hard knuckles of driftwood, and the way the spines of the bushes catch at hair and brush along an arm like a long-nailed hand. She knows how it's possible to find oneself trapped in a cul-de-sac in the dry bushes, in some spot where a barrage of wood and flotsam was jammed between branches during the last spring tide, and how it is necessary to double back and try another path through the scrub. The progress of the two children is erratic, but they are moving steadily closer to the man, whose body is completely still in the sunlight except for his hands, invisible behind the bushes but busy as if with a stiff belt buckle.

Many small rooms surrounded the huge central space in which lengths of rusty chain swayed slowly from the ceiling far above, and the old warehouse reeked of the forbidden, of all those warnings from Mum. The chains could have been swaying from the habit of earlier days, when they hung weighted with loads and moved at the shouts of muscular men, or it might have been just a trick of the blood rushing to the head as Louise tilted her head back to look up dizzily at the rafters, almost invisible in the dusty gloom overhead. Through holes in the roof, sunlight slanted down, heavy with dust and warming small patches of the greasy floorboards so that a strong smell of hot oil rose from each patch of sunlight. The silence here throbbed in Louise's ears and she held her breath and stared at Kevin.

— Just a dirty old place, she said and glanced around, surprised at the loud wavering quality of her voice.

— You're scared, Kevin said, and turned as if to go. Having established that Louise was frightened, it seemed that he could now go back to the clean sun outside, and games in air that moved and breathed instead of hanging thick with dust and the smell of dead machines.

— We've got to get a souvenir, Louise said, trying to speak more softly so that this time her voice would not shake the hushed air, and finding that instead her voice was a breathy whisper.

— A what?

Kevin was also whispering and he glanced around as if checking that the broken window they'd come in by was still there.

— A souvenir. You know, proof.

There was nothing on the rotting wooden work-benches but a thick layer of dust which formed a greasy ball when Louise ran a finger through it.

— Nothing here, said Kevin. Nothing here. Let's go.

Louise saw how he stood in the very middle of the space, as far as possible from any shadowed corner where things might be crouching and watching. She spoke loudly as if to warn any lurking creature to retreat:

108

— You go then, scaredy-cat. Wait outside then.

Feeling him follow her, but at a distance, she walked out of the well-lit centre of the warehouse into the shadows where doors opened reluctantly into small rooms like cells. In these rooms the smell of oil and rotten wood was overlaid by a rich organic scent of animal decay, and the silence sang in Louise's ears like the noise inside a shell. In the second room, Kevin stepped into a coil of turd which crumbled under his sandal, and he gasped as if bitten. The windows in these rooms were heavily boarded and the thin bands of sun that penetrated between the planks lit up stiff clumps of rag and brown-smeared newspapers, and made a green bottle gleam like an eye. The six brass nails, new but without heads, which they found on the bench in this room seemed enough of a souvenir, and, feeling them grow warm in her hand, Louise made her way quickly back into the open space where the chains seemed to be swaying faster now, as if to throw themselves in a long weighty arc over the children beneath. Lit up by a single crisp bar of sunlight, a loop of metal sat on the floor like a snake and above it on the wall Louise read a daubed word.

— F-L-I-C-K, she spelled out. What's that mean, FLICK?

Kevin stared at it and she watched his lips moving as they always did when he read. As he mouthed the last letter she saw him understand.

— What's it mean Kevin? Why'd they write FLICK?

He glanced at her and pursed his lips the way the teachers did when they wanted you to guess.

— You're so smart, he said. Work it out for yourself.

He ran across to the broken window and for a moment Louise felt alone in the middle of this silent space. She watched the soles of his sandals as Kevin crawled out, and waited until they were both standing outside before she put the brass nails ostentatiously into her own pocket, without offering to share them. She found herself shouting into the air outside, here where cicadas shrilled from trees and grasshoppers leapt out of the dry grass with a crackling like fire. She felt the breeze blow in her face and was aware of every hair on her body standing erect.

— Come on, tell me, come on, Louise shouted at Kevin's silent face, and it was some moments before she turned and saw the old man behind her.

In the shadow under the brim of the dark hat, one eye was completely closed and Louise watched a fly crawl towards the other eye, which was pale as if boiled and leaked shining tears. One large hand was waving towards her as if trying to locate her by touch. *Come on closer come on.* Louise saw his tongue, pink in the darkness of his mouth. *Closer where I can see you, closer.* Louise backed step by step against the wall of the warehouse and felt the heat it threw out into her back, and its splinters in her palms. *Don't be scared come closer come on.* The wall had stored up a whole summer's heat and smelled of creosote and ants. *Where are you be nice to a poor old man now.* His clothes were dark and dense and as he reached towards her again she smelt sweaty hot serge and felt splinters in her back. His other hand came out of a pocket and thrust close to her face. *Look, nice lollies have a nice lolly put your hand in go on.* His trousers close to her face were hot and huge and the small paper bag was greying along its creases. The enormous hand moved and she saw the bag fall to the ground and two shiny red lollies bounced and came to rest. She felt the hand take hold of her shoulder, covering it with immediate damp heat, and felt his breath on her cheek and could see the shiny white of his eye in the shadow of his hat. *Yes yes closer yes.* She felt her shoulder cool as the hand left it and brushed down to where her shorts ended. The hand slid up and down her leg and she felt the heat in her back as she squirmed away from the puffs of breath on her face and the hoarse voice rasping *yes yes here we go yes*. The thumb slid up under the cloth of her shorts and she felt it jabbing and probing into her, harder and harder between her legs until the man grunted and the thumb was abruptly withdrawn. She turned her cheek against the splinters and smelled the creosote as she drew in a long quivering breath.

When she opened her eyes again she saw the man turning in a crouch towards Kevin who was standing shocked and still, with a hand up to his mouth. The man reached out with both groping hands, whispering urgently, *the boy, come on sonnie where are you now*. Louise felt the splinters catch at her shirt as she straightened against the wall and saw the dark hat with its darker band of sweat hovering over Kevin's wide eyes and the huge exploring hand fumbling down towards the front of his shorts. The man took a clumsy shuffling step closer to Kevin and Louise saw the red lolly crushed into shiny chips under his heel.

The boat wallows and staggers in the water as Louise digs down hard with an oar and the slithering weight of the jellyfish on the floorboards slips to one side. Now that she is rowing towards him, she can no longer watch the man, but takes a glimpse over her shoulder after every few strokes and tries to keep her course straight towards him. She sees him bend behind the bushes and pull as if at a trouser-leg and along the sea-wall the children are darting between the bushes, always looking behind them at where the dog whines and claws at the fence, never looking ahead to where the man is standing now with his hands at his waist behind the bushes. Louise takes only a glance before bending to the oars again and wonders how close she will have to be before she can call out to the children.

The jellyfish in the bottom of the boat are shedding their first layers of slime so that the water that slops over her feet is full of long slippery strands. Her palms against the leather grips of the oars are sticky with dried jelly and a floury damp smell rises from the floor. At her next twisted glance over her shoulder she is close enough to see the man's dark eye-sockets, shadowed by the sun, and sees his watchband glint again as he raises his arm as if in farewell to the children, who have turned without ever catching sight of him, and are making their way back towards the fence. They throw dried seaweed at each other as they run along the sea-wall and Louise hears the splash as a clump lands in the water and one of the children begins to shriek.

Along the waterline on the sea-wall, bright green weed floats like hair and at each deep insuck of the swell, fleshy brown kelp washes into view for a moment seething and coiling. The man no longer even glances in the direction of the children's cries, but stares at Louise intently as if trying telepathy. As she sits holding the oars blankly, he beckons her with imperious gestures that make his watchband wink in rapid semaphore, and begins to move towards her through the bushes. Holding branches carefully away from his body, he advances steadily towards her as if planning to march straight across the water to where she now struggles to get the heavy boat moving. As he bends back the last branch that hides him from her, his stare opens into a grin that exposes every tooth and the shining pink end of a wet tongue. He continues to stare directly into her eyes and she has to stare back as she propels herself away from him with convulsive jerks on the oars, feeling her palms slip on the leather grips and long fibrous threads squeezing between her toes.

No Such Thing as a Free Lunch

It's a fancy place in the way places are fancy here. Dim yellowish walls which anywhere else you might take the liberty of calling shabby. Ah — but the paintings! One doesn't like to look naive and peer too closely, but clearly they're originals, little gems dashed off by the masters, signed with a flourish. My compliments to the chef and to Claude for his wonderful restaurant. The lights are dim but of course no mere vulgar pink. This, my dear, is the dimness of quality. Among the sparkling white linen and the shadowy old chairs — old but good — large elegant men sit back at ease with a bottle of de Rothschild still half full in front of them. Poised women sparkle discreetly, leaning languorously, laughing in streams of silver bells.

Oliver does not, of course, expect me to exclaim aloud my awe or to shame him by clumsy colonial enthusiasm. Super cool now behind the black cummerbund of the maitre de. Skirt round this chair, don't brush the tablecloth as you pass and for heaven's sake try not to knock those flowers over. Chin up, back straight, now. No scurrying. Well done.

The chair is being pulled out for me and the oily face

inclining with bogus respect. Madame? Slide in slowly now. Weight on the balls of the feet so that he can slide the chair in under me. Well done. What a team.

Oliver is of course totally au fait and absolutely au courant with this place. Evening Luigi, how are you this evening glad to hear it. Where's Claude tonight I don't see him. A few new faces I see. Well now what do you recommend tonight Luigi? The plovers' eggs in sauce de la maison? Plovers' eggs it shall be. That is, unless, of course . . . he inclines his smooth polished Public School face towards me . . . no that will be fine Luigi, two plovers' eggs. And I think a bottle of the '68 don't you? Yes. Fine.

Of course I come here pretty often you know. The odd business lunch and pleasurable um dinner. Nice quiet place. Bit pricey of course but utterly worth every penny.

At the next table a young man with pale eyes like a blind fish in a dead-white hairless face is talking steadily, calmly, without the slightest shadow of a doubt, to his companion who is elegant in black silk and blond coiffure. Her perfect face framed in the bell of her hair stares at him. She nods, murmurs. Absolutely oh yes. Quite. How amusing. Quite. Her dark eyes never leave his decomposing-flesh face. Oh how splendid. How absolutely. She leans forward to him, one hand supporting an elegant cheekbone, the other resting, forefinger pointing, on the table.

Oliver unfolds his napkin and arranges it in his lap.

Now we were talking were we not about *Lear*, without a doubt the greatest play ever written. Genius with a capital G. That strange quality not so very far from madness which we like to call Genius.

His voice is properly reverent in the face of Genius with a capital G.

I venture to differ. *Hamlet*, perhaps?

Oh no dear. You're quite wrong about that. Without any argument his masterwork, his chef d'oeuvre as it were. Definitely his greatest. No. I was just talking to Hall about this very subject last week and he was telling me. No, I'd say you'll have to look at it again. Ah the wine thanks Luigi.

The correct half-inch in the glass. Lift it to the light and peer at it with one eye. Swill it round in the glass. Sniff. Close eyes the better to appreciate this really remarkably fine aroma. Tilt the head back, toss it in and swill it around the back teeth before finally swallowing. Purse the lips. Yes lovely. Not quite up to the '65 naturally but what would you?

At the next table the food has arrived. The long slender fingers delicately grasp the knife and fork and convey dainty morsels to the perfect mouth. Chewing discreetly, she nods and leans forward, swan-like, between mouthfuls, all intelligent interest. Her companion picks petulantly at his food and lifts a disdainful forkful to the blank hole of his mouth.

Well now what were we saying yes the Theatre. Of course the Theatre is without a doubt the highest form of art. No doubt that a fine piece of theatre played by truly professional actors well there's nothing can touch it in terms of sheer artistry. Now the films. I know you work in the films. Well I'm sure there's a lot of merit in certain films but you won't convince me that it's a medium in which art can flourish. Fine for a night's simple entertainment of course absolutely. Quite hits the spot at certain times. And of course for the mass of people, the bulk of the population, well I don't of course want to sound snobbish or in the slightest degree elitist but I'm sure you'll understand when I say that some pleasures require an educated palate.

Another swig of wine hits his educated palate and he closes his eyes and leans back.

Now what would you call a really good film, I mean a film that's not simply a piece of entertainment now I did see a good film a while ago, what was the name of it now. Remarkably fine film within the limitations of the medium. Now a film like that takes the medium to its highest point and there's no doubt there's a lot of merit in it, without a doubt that film is one of the masterworks of that particular medium. But compare it with a piece of true theatre and you'll just have to agree with me.

The plovers' eggs arrive and look distinctly nasty.

I think you'll find that these are really remarkably fine. You'll enjoy these, no question of it.

Now you're obviously an intelligent girl I'd be interested to hear your views on this. Clearly you're not just a run of the mill type of person. Obviously you're more intelligent than most and I'll be interested in your opinion. Now the way I see it is this, you've got two distinct and separate things going on and only one of them can rightly be called Art. And of course there's not a shadow of a doubt in my mind that.

The plovers' eggs are like the insides of golf balls.

Yes the chef here really is remarkably fine no-one to touch him in the whole of London. Now I was talking to Claude last week and I said Claude your chef is a treasure. I think you'll agree that this is the finest food of its kind you've ever tasted.

Absolutely tip top Luigi up to the usual high standard do convey my felicitations to Pierre. I think you'll have to agree that burp. Pardon me.

Now if you'll just excuse me a moment. Bows slightly the embodiment of breeding.

The dead fish at the next table is also making his way to the door at the back. When he's out of sight the immaculate blond slumps forward at the table and covers her face with her hands. Under the table I see her kick off a shoe and scratch the back of her leg with her toes. She sits for a few moments with her face in her hands hidden by the bell of her hair. She looks up at last, straightens her back, resumes the graceful listening attitude, takes a sip of wine. She catches my eye. Without cracking the perfect symmetry and beauty of her heart-shaped face, she gives me a slow patient wink from one brown eye. Then with a wide pink cat's mouth she yawns — tremendously, tonsil-exposingly, eloquently.

Country Pleasures

Tomb-violators start by whispering and end by shouting and smashing the hieroglyphs, cursing the priests who might have mixed smallpox with the mortar between the stones. When Rennie and Louise began exploring the house they tiptoed and were unable to understand each other. *What? Find something?* Each room they entered was dark and not quite silent but when the shutters were pushed back against the clenched hinges, yellow Tuscan light filled the air and revealed nothing more sinister than a scattering of mouse-droppings on the floor. Under the decayed ceiling of the middle room upstairs, a heap of acid-white guano represented years of life in the dove-loft in the roof. Next door in the corner room, the shutters had surrendered to a push and fallen away smoothly into the bushes outside, leaving the window-frame to sag inwards like a drunk needing a friend. Rennie and Louise stepped quickly back and glanced up at the dark beams above them that supported the roof. The adze marks of two centuries before could still be seen on the dry flaky wood, but the deep fissures running the length of the beams were more recent. Along these flaws the colossal weight of the terracotta tiles was bearing down, teasing the grain of the wood further and further apart, towards the final collapse that would send clouds of dust and astonished doves into the air. Rennie left the room in haste and Louise followed, stepping gingerly across the loose crunching tiles as if quiet footsteps weighed less than noisy ones.

Of the six rooms upstairs, they decided to use only the two where furniture stood crookedly on the tiles, and left the others to breathe and crumble quietly behind closed doors. In the back room with the murkily mirrored wardrobe, they swept up the mouse-droppings and used the ornate hangers from the Hotel Palazzo Moderno.

Along the hall in what came to be called the Embryo Room, Rennie stamped experimentally on the floor, glanced up at the ceiling where a few flakes of plaster drifted down, and decided that this was the best room to work in. As well as the table which he dragged over to the window to use as a desk, there were three narrow beds in the room, each with a tight cover of clear plastic over the mattress. The middle bed was home for a colony of mice whose nest under the plastic was exposed like the cross-section of a termite-riddled log. Four mouselings, like thick pink maggots, seethed slowly over each other in the centre of the nest while the adult mice rooted further into the wadding among the springs, enlarging the hole. In spite of the transparent plastic, the mice thought they were invisible, not at all disturbed by the bulky shapes bending over them.

— Wonderful. Tremendously good omen.

Rennie held Louise with one arm around her waist while with the stubby forefinger of the other he crinkled the plastic over the nest. The mice stopped their shifting over each other and froze as if listening.

— All this new life. All this fruition.

Louise nodded in agreement and pressed up and down on the mattress so the nest swayed and bounced like a bottle at sea and the mice scrabbled at each other, clawing over each other's backs. One slipped up out of the hole and slid along between the plastic and the mattress towards the edge of the bed. With her hands on either side of the mouse, tightening the plastic, Louise watched its fur flatten, saw the tiny head struggle, and waited until it resigned itself to immobility, only the long tail twitching like the ones lizards leave behind. When she took her hands away it turned and crept swiftly back into the nest on top of the mouselings. How sweetly he'd kiss her, *Darling, that's wonderful*, and what a smile he'd give her. *With any luck it'll be a little girl like you*. How easy it was to imagine the bewilderment, *But of course we want to keep it*, and to feel his eyes watching her.

— Darling don't miss this view.

Below the house, a patchy field of wheat like a badly-shaved cheek ran down to the wood in the valley, and a matching field ran up the other side to the house on the opposite hill. The symmetry was perfect, except for the white curtain lolling like a tongue out of a window in the other house. It seemed possible to walk out of this window in a straight line across the air into the same window across the valley, where the curtain shifted along the wall from time to time. Rennie and Louise stood watching in silence as if hoping to see their neighbours appear, and when Rennie turned away from the window it was as if in pique that they hadn't.

— Got a bit of cleaning ahead of us.

He kicked at a crumpled sheet of newspaper beside the table, revealing a small hole in the wall at floor-level, surrounded like a rabbit's burrow with a scattering of sandy mortar from the interior of the wall.

— Must be the mice.

He bent down, peering closely, and pushed a finger in, but drew it out again quickly as if remembering childhood warnings about the perils of fingers in holes.

— I like to imagine them coming and going while I work.

He pulled the paper back loosely over the hole and stood looking at it.

Even after they'd beaten, aired and swept for a week they still gave the furniture a few kicks before sitting down, and small humped shapes could still be seen moving furtively under the loose covers. Rennie refused to go near the couch, but Louise enjoyed the flurry when she sat down and four or five grey blurs shot out of the hole in the back, leaving a hairy trail of stuffing, and whirred along the skirting-board towards the gap under the door. The first night they spent in the house, Rennie lay awake waiting for the tiny feet on his face, and next day insisted that the legs of the bed be set in deep bowls of water. Then he expected to hear the squeaks and desperate splashings of a drowning mouse, and propped the legs and bowls up on boxes. Louise had to watch as he strained and swore, sending the bowls reeling across the tiles but refusing help. Afterwards he lay as if after a debilitating illness while she brought him tea and massaged his back. Each time she found it harder to resist using her nails to tear off the bulbous black mole under his shoulder blade.

At night Louise listened to the soft scrapings and patterings throughout the house. Rennie breathed heavily beside her and the bedclothes stirred regularly over his rounded back, but she wondered whether he was really asleep. If she whispered *Fire*, would he spring upright, fling the bedclothes back, leap to the window? The bed was almost too narrow for a couple, but even so Rennie managed to make a space between their bodies as they slept. When Louise slid across the bed to shape herself against his back, he retreated further to the very edge of the bed, so she wondered how he balanced. She slid back to her own side of the bed and lay with her hands under her head, considering grossly obese women and their reinforced mattresses. When they feel the urge to turn in bed from one massive hip to the other, their tiny husbands are forced to slide to the floor, pad around the bed, and get in on the other side. In the larger bed, at home in London, it had been less obvious that there was easily room for a third body to lie between the husband and wife.

Each thick beam of the ceiling had once been an entire tree twisting up towards the light and thrusting puny ones aside to wither in the shade, and the shape of each individual struggle could still be seen against the white plaster. The impression was one of massive vegetable strength. However, each evening before climbing up into the bed, Louise and Rennie shook the pillows and blankets, sneezing in the fine cloud of grit they disturbed. Throughout the day, tiny flakes of plaster detached themselves from the ceiling and floated down like dandruff, while grains of sawdust fell from the thousands of pin-point holes that riddled the beams. Louise knew that the light rain of debris must fall during the night as well as the day, and in the morning their faces must be covered like the pillows with grit. How long would it take, lying without motion, to be hidden like a rock under snow? Perhaps before that, the whole house would gracefully fold in on itself, in that surprisingly lingering way a building will fall to its knees when subjected to the wrong kind of stress.

Through the still house the scrabble of claws over tiles carried clearly, like the tiny manic scratch of a watch held to the ear. Louise fingered the damp warmth between her legs, closing her eyes and seeing the inquisitive noses twitching, the whiskers quivering knowingly, the eyes alert and unblinking in the darkness. Only her hand moved, rasping regularly against the sheet, and her breath came quickly but softly until her knees weakened and fell away from each other. She lay still with a hand warming her belly. Even back in London she'd known how to set the bed squeaking and to create such a friction in the space between their bodies that she could no longer believe that Rennie was asleep. But these days, in this bed where any movement made the water slosh in the bowls, she preferred to move silently and pretend that her husband was unaware of what her hand was doing. Holding her breath she listened to his steady exhalations and imagined his eyes wide in the dark, fixed on the gray of the window, concentrating on keeping his breathing as unhurried as a true sleeper's. Louise jammed her forefinger up into herself as far as it would go, then held it to her face, straining to see, sniffing, finally licking tentatively with the tip of her tongue. There was still no sign, no stickiness, no sharp metallic taste. She lay very still, wondering how much longer Rennie would fail to notice the gap in the rhythm of her months, hoping that nothing would make him guess at the possibility of a new being embedded in her flesh, swelling on her blood, waiting to come out.

In the morning a dead curled mouse floated stiffly in one of the bowls and the loose wallpaper in the next room flapped erratically like someone preparing to speak and thinking better of it.

— Oh Louise I love you, Rennie said as he did every morning, propped up on his elbow in the bed, the brown nightshirt hiked around his waist.

— I love you too, she said, her lips shaping themselves stiffly around the words. Outside, Domenico clapped his hands together and made abrupt barking sounds while the goat's feet clattered and slipped on the flagstones. She stared into Rennie's eyes silently trying it backwards, *uoy evol i.*

— You look so far away, what are you thinking?

She didn't say, of how this roof could cave in and how that beam would crush you like a cockroach.

— I'm wondering what that big hook up there was for, she said, and he finally looked away from her at the ceiling.

— Hanging hares or hams or something. Or maybe Daniel hanged his wife.

Her laughter set up a tiny soft squeak in the bed as its old joints moved against each other, and she slid over to Rennie's side of the bed, feeling her bare thigh against his and reaching down with an exploring hand. Her mouth touched his at the same moment that her fingers brushed into his groin and he arched away from both points of contact like a hooked fish. He rubbed his lips hard as if stung.

— Ticklish. That tickled.

He gave her a fleeting dry kiss on the neck before turning away from her, knees together like a modest girl, and throwing back the covers as if letting light into a darkly curtained room. Once out of bed, the heavy nightshirt falling as far as his ankles, he bent down to kiss her mouth, but when she tried to pull him closer he straightened up out of the embrace. As he pulled on his shorts and running shoes his face was without expression. Louise pulled her nightgown up to her armpits and ran her hands over her waist.

— Am I putting on weight? Am I getting old and ugly?

Her smile indicated the answer she expected, but, with

one foot up on a box tying the lace, he looked her over as if literally calculating.

— No darling. Lovely as ever.

He turned to the wardrobe while she lay watching him line up the shirt carefully to get the right buttons in the right holes, then impatiently she dragged the sheet up from her toes and over her head, an old-fashioned corpse. He combed his hair before turning to the bed, seeming not to notice the shroud, and squeezed her foot through the sheet.

— See you a bit later darling.

His rubber soles squeaked down the stairs and across the living room, and the hens set up a panicked clucking and flapping as he disturbed them outside the front door. Louise flung the sheet back as she heard Rennie call out good morning to Domenico, and thrust her fingers up into herself one more time. They were still unstained.

Sitting up in the bed with an abrupt movement that made the wooden boxes creak, she took off her nightgown and threw it down on the floor beside the bed, listening for a moment before sliding down. As she reached for her shoes on the top of the wardrobe the mirrored door swung open and like a magician's trick revealed the clothes hanging inside and a scattering of mouse-droppings beside her galoshes. She checked the pockets of her skirt before putting it on and going downstairs, feeling last night's droppings on the landing crush underfoot.

Passing through the rest of the house and entering the kitchen was as much a shock as the faultlessly toothed smile in some collapsing old face. It was the only room that had been renovated when work on the house had been abandoned, and its efficiency and purity were so daunting that every clot of tomato pulp on the white counters was a violation. While the rest of the house had hardly even a minimum of equipment, this room was prepared for any possible operation with spatulas, graters, whisks like the diagram of an atom, blenders, mixers, dicers. In each drawer the knives lay like dentists' tools in their trays — the smiling curved ones for grapefruit, the businesslike ones for steak, the fish knives with a nick in each blade like a shark's undershot jaw. The only decorations in the room were the rows of steel choppers and slicers, each clinging to its small magnet on the wall. At the end of the row, the massive square cleaver hung like an overgrown awkward child stooping bashfully and round-shouldered beside his shorter classmates. The row of small knives for vegetables was arranged in a crescent, the long slim slicers taking up position on the edges like those actors who stand throughout a scene on either side of the stage, holding up a spear. Between them were the small knives for paring and coring and opening oysters. Louise had never before used a kitchen with more than at most two knives sharp enough for anything but bread-and-butter. Now she bought tough stewing meat so as to use the heavy choppers, took delight in shattering chicken carcasses with the gross blunt-nosed cleaver, and would have bought oysters if she could.

Domenico came to the front door throwing a long shadow across the tiles into the kitchen, holding the loaf at his side half-hidden as if he planned to produce it suddenly like a snake out of a handkerchief.

— Buon giorno, Domenico, come sta?

Domenico bent forward like a runner and grinned so the white stubble folded into the grooves beside his mouth. He held the bread out without coming closer and as she took hold of one end he continued holding the other while telling her what good bread it was. How it was good because it was not salted. How he would bring it again not tomorrow (with elaborate hand-over-hand gestures), but the day after tomorrow, and how did she like Italy? Because of his lack of teeth and the explosive way he brought out his words, and because of her rudimentary Italian, for the first week Louise had just nodded and smiled. Now she knew their conversation word for word and only had to listen for the pauses. *Si, si, mi piace l'Italia. Grazie tante.* Domenico stretched his lips over his sunken mouth and hovered as if to say more, but instead made his leave-taking gresture, a circling of a flat-palmed hand like polishing a pane of glass between them. A flurry of hens agitated after him for their morning scattering of grain as he walked back across the yard to his barn.

Louise picked out a grapefruit from the basket, feeling the saliva gush into her mouth at the thought of the tart juice. Neither Louise nor Rennie was very fond of grapefruit, but she bought them these days because of the knives, and relished the way the two halves fell away from the blade, and the way the left-handed grapefruit knife enabled her to sever the pith from the fruit in two slices.

— Darling it's such a splendid day.

Rennie stood blocking the sun in the doorway, glowing from his jog. When she turned to him their smiles collided across the room. His face was featureless against the bright sky.

— That's wonderful, she said. Maybe we could have our walk a bit early today.

The blade continued to split off each segment of fruit from the next while she heard the words steaming effortlessly off the top of her thoughts. Rennie spoke with the special jovial voice he kept for children and geriatrics.

— How's Domenico this morning? Still getting the bread through? Pretty fair hike for an old chap like him.

He bent and stretched in the doorway, touching his toes

and straightening again methodically. Louise saw him lined up with the other boys in the huge greenish gym, panting, guffawing, wrestling later, falling against the lockers.

— Yes, but he's probably fitter than you or me.

Seeming not to hear her, Rennie straightened up one last time and stood, feet apart, jerking his elbows back at chest height, hands level beneath his chin. *I must, I must, increase my bust*, she used to snicker with the other girls, all in their bottle-green bloomers, thrusting their elbows back hard and giggling. Arriving at the final ritual, Rennie's eyes were closed as if in ecstasy while he rolled his head around on his shoulders, circling his face back and around with swooning abandon. In pregnancy, nipples turned brown, breasts engorged and blue veins wound across their curves, and the whole pelvis spread so that the shiny head could force its way out into the light, covered with blood, bawling.

They sat on opposite sides of the huge marble-topped table that dominated the kitchen. She'd laid a tea-towel in front of each chair, hanging over the edge of the table, because the deep chill of the marble had numbed their wrists. Some days Louise still found her fingers searching for the shallow gutter that she expected to find grooved into the marble around the edge. Rennie's face puckered at the first mouthful of fruit, but he gobbled it quickly, swallowing each segment whole. Louise ate steadily, keeping her face unmoved and staring at the streaked white marble thinking not about grapefruit but of baclava oozing with honey, of chocolate, of the soft dripping pulp of an over-ripe mango raised to the mouth with one hand while the other waves away the circling bee. She laid her spoon down with a sigh when every shred of the bitter fruit was eaten.

— You never liked these before, what made you change?

Smiling, Louise shook her head, staring at Rennie but picturing a chill shuttered room with a tiled floor and herself standing in front of the desk before some dome-headed doctor, stumbling in Italian and finally, obscenely, gesturing what she meant. It would be necessary to bend her knees and point them outwards like a frozen Charleston and make ushering or pulling gestures with her hands. He could probably have her arrested.

— Well darling, up to the salt mines for me.

Rennie wiped his mouth with the tea-towel, and, as if gazing into a mirror, smoothed his moustache with a caressing gesture. *My husband*, Louise reminded herself. *My husband*.

She continued to sit staring at the scooped pith shells, listening to his heavy feet go up the stairs and along the passage, first to the bathroom to shower away the sweat of his run, then to the Embryo Room above her head where his chair scraped along the floor as he sat at the desk and drew towards him the notes on *Jeremy Bentham: The Life and The Work of*. When he'd finished the book, when he'd received the doctorate, when they were Dr and Mrs Dufrey — then, he implied, their life would really start. Louise heard the clink of the *Acqua Minerale* bottle against the glass and could imagine him take a mouthful of water, throw his head back and gargle briefly and loudly before spitting out the window, burping and uncapping the fountain pen.

Standing at the sink washing the breakfast dishes, Louise could not see the whole of the house on the other hill, as Rennie did from his desk above her. But the upper storey was visible above the trees, and the flagpole Daniel had told them about, where a small triangular flag usually fluttered, like the ones that mean *Customs Officer Aboard* or *In Quarantine* that ships fly when coming into port. Some days not one, but several flags flew from the pole, and on those days Louise and Rennie tried to imagine what the flags must mean for Gabriel and Elena, Daniel's children. Did they spell out a message, and if so, for whom?

Because of the provisional, half-renovated state of the house, furniture was sparse, and the table Rennie used was the only kind of desk. Louise had to make sure that her chair was standing securely on the middle of the coffee table before climbing up carefully into it and pulling the typewriter towards her on top of the dresser, nearly five feet off the ground, where she worked. Beside the typewriter was yesterday's carbon copy of another chapter of *Jeremy Bentham: The Life and The Work of*, ready to be mailed back to London in case of some Act of God in Tuscany. Louise was momentarily appalled at the number of fires that would have to take place all over Europe for the entire oeuvre to be lost. She took out a fresh sheet of carbon paper and started to type, hesitating often at a word and mouthing possibilities like someone prompting a ouija board. In the quiet house, the erratic din of the typewriter seemed very loud in spite of the folded towel Rennie had suggested she put under the machine. *It just echoes right up the stairs darling. I know it's not your fault but it's terrifically hard to concentrate.* For herself, Louise had enjoyed the angry clatter of the machine, efficient and indifferent like a mechanical cookie-cutter.

Because of Rennie's scribbles and corrections, and rewritten corrections of corrections, it was impossible not to read the words she was typing and absorb their meaning. Was that why she made so many mistakes, why she typed Bent ham and swore at least twice on every page? Was that why, once or more a day, she wanted to heave the typewriter against the wall? Was that why she typed for an hour without once checking, as she knew she should, that the back legs of the chair were not inching off the coffee table? As the weeks had passed, Rennie's notes had become more and more overscrawled, more embroidered with asterisks, arrows, elaborate instructions for reversing sentences, and each day there was a page or two less to type.

Rennie complained easily of distractions these days, and she knew not to run the hot water while he was working, not to do the dishes with gusto but furtively, placing each plate in the rack as carefully as priceless Ming to prevent one plate clinking against another, and not to blow her nose in the house, but to take herself outside to do it, watched in amazement by the goat. Rennie complained that the doves, in the loft above him, made a terrific racket, but there was nothing they could do about that. When Domenico shouted to the animals, or started one of his loud monologues in the barn, Rennie would bite his pen, the frown deepening on his face until he flung the chair back with an angry scrape, and paced around the room, startling the mice. Only when Domenico fell silent would work on *Jeremy Bentham: The Life and The Work of* start again.

The barn where Domenico lived in pungent dusk with the animals was a squat stone structure that would probably outlast the house by a couple of centuries. His voice emerged muffled through the fortress-like walls, but when his pacing took him close to the door, the staccato shouting carried clearly across the yard to the house. The animals must have accustomed themselves to sharing their space with these harangues, and in fact for Louise, watching and listening from her perch by the window, it seemed that their comings and goings were dictated by his speeches and silences. She strained to hear, but his toothless colloquialisms were incomprehensible to her even when a phrase or two carried intact across the yard. In the silence that followed a burst of words, while she imagined him listening to the reply, the doves swept down from the loft as if at a signal, their slow wings making a sound like unoiled hinges. They settled along the top of the crumbling stone arch near the barn, a relic of some even more ancient building. When they had rearranged themselves with a few quick flutterings into the air and down again, Domenico's voice rose in a chant that could have been *si, per favore, si, per favore, si si.* His voice cracked and, as if they had been waiting for this, the doves all spread their wings and dropped down to the stubble field beneath. *Prego, prego, prego!* Domenico called out on a rising inflexion like despair, and a line of hens ran quickly out of the barn and across the yard. Dull wooden sounds as of light furniture being shifted carried faintly across the yard. Like an inquisitor listing transgressions, Domenico held forth again, in that resonant, imperious voice he used only in the privacy of the barn.

Louise finished typing the last page of Rennie's notes and was shuffling them together in a neat pile when she heard a rustle outside the open window and the goat's Chinaman face blinked in at her like an inquisitive neighbour. After staring at her and at everything on the dresser, the goat vanished from the window, but a moment later it hesitated at the front door, sniffing the air as if for a trap, then clopped briskly across the tiles to the dresser. Ignoring Louise, it placed its front hooves up on the coffee table with the delicacy of a circus pony, and reached with its whiskery lips for the roses in the jar beside the typewriter. The coarse beard wagged as it enveloped each flower in its mouth and munched before reaching for the next. With each rose gobbled, it shot a sideways glance at Louise.

When the roses were finished it let itself back down onto the floor, where it discovered a small paper bag and was munching that, blinking, when Domenico's face appeared framed in the window. He exclaimed indignantly, gesturing at the goat, and a thread of spittle landed on Rennie's notes. Crouching as if hiding in long grass, he half-ran through the doorway towards the goat, making a grab for the rope round the animal's neck. The goat ducked and skittered sideways, trotting round the room before leaping onto the sofa, its wicked eyes rolling. Domenico hissed and barked at it, finally making a lunge across the sofa and grabbing the rope with a hoarse shout.

— What the hell's going on, what's all the noise?

Rennie's hand rested on the knob of the bannister like the lord of the manor and Louise turned carefully in her chair to watch her husband's annoyance. In the silence in which they all stared at each other, the goat lowered its head obstinately against the rope and let fall a few dry turds that made a light patter on the tiles. Domenico let go of the rope and sent the goat out the door with a slap on its bony behind. He scuffed the turds under the table with the side of his boot, then looked up to show his sunken grin to Rennie as if nothing had happened.

— Buon giorno, he mumbled ingratiatingly.

Rennie came down the last step and frowned more deeply as he said:

— Buon giorno, Domenico.

Each letter was painfully distinct so that he sounded emphatically English.

— Louise, we've got to tell him we can't have this. Domenico, io, er, scrivo. Non posso scrivere . . .

He turned to Louise.

— We've got to tell him, he said crossly.

— But darling, he was getting rid of it for us.

Her words hung in the silence like a plea and when Domenico murmured *mi scusi, mi scusi*, with a placating gesture, Louise and the old man seemed joined like scolded children against Rennie. He glanced from his wife to Domenico like someone cornered, then came forward smiling quickly and saying:

— Okay Domenico. Ah . . .

He turned to Louise.

— How do I say it's okay?

— Va bene.

— Va bene, Rennie repeated. Um . . . how do I say thanks for getting rid of it?

Louise shrugged and turned to Domenico.

— Grazie per . . . she made the shooing gestures Domenico had used to drive out the goat.

She saw how black and toothless the inside of his mouth was when he opened it in a silent laugh and shuffled towards the door with vague bowing gestures. The chair that Louise used to prop open the front door caught his eye and he seemed unable to resist stopping, running a hand over the seat like a caress, and lifting it as if to judge its weight.

— Ciao, Louise called.

He straightened up guiltily from the chair and quickly polished a small area of glass between them before leaving, with one last glance at the chair. Rennie flipped through the papers on the dresser.

— This footnote's a bit out of line, he pointed out. But you're doing a tremendous job, darling.

He stretched and yawned.

— God I get so stiff. Hard labour up there.

He touched her hair briefly as if testing its temperature.

— How about you darling. Watch this chair, now.

He shifted the chair with Louise in it closer to the centre of the coffee table.

— This is a different chair again isn't it? Did that old fruitcake make off with another one?

As he finished speaking, Domenico's other voice rang out from the barn, the words unclear but the tone one of command — sonorous, pounding rhetoric that could convert souls and lead armies into battle.

— Think we should tell Gabriel? They're kind of his chairs.

Louise shook her head and said:

— I don't think he could care less.

Rennie nodded indifferently and Louise watched his cheeks shake as he began to run on the spot, lifting his knees high. Moving geometrically like an athlete on an amphora, he ran once around the room, paused to give Louise a kiss on her shoulder, then ran up the stairs two at a time. When they'd first arrived, they'd moved around the house quietly, as if a sleeper must not be disturbed, and Rennie had often fallen silent in the middle of a sentence and stared at Louise, holding his breath, listening. Now Louise heard the stairway tremble under his weight, and imagined a few more cracks in the risers, and the beams shifting apart another fraction of an inch. Daniel had described the house as rustic and had apologized for offering it to them for the summer, but both Rennie and Louise had assumed this to be a self-deprecating understatement, and had expected much turned and varnished wood, bunches of dried flowers in every corner, and perhaps even the charming anachronism of a well in the centre of an overgrown garden. They had not thought that Daniel's description was actually a euphemism for terminal decay.

After the long drive of wrong turns taken through three countries, and directions asked of wooden-faced locals gesturing towards the hills ahead, they'd found that the key Daniel had given them in London no longer turned in the lock. With an uncomfortable feeling of being watched, they pushed through the blackberry bushes around the house until they found a window small enough to break without guilt but wide enough for Louise to crawl through. *Careful*, Rennie repeated as she took hold of the rotten frame to pull herself up. *Careful now.* Her palm had brushed something cool and slick. She held the cut on the side of her hand, half-crouching in a dank room listening to the soft foreign noises of the house.

They'd asked for Varetto, as Daniel had told them to, but the sun-hardened farmers, and their wives holding aprons full of peas, had shaken their heads blankly. At last Rennie had lost patience with these peasants who refused to understand him, and had driven fast and furious along the narrow lanes, turning to right and left at random, trusting to some magic to bring them to their destination. It was only at the top of a hill, seeing for the third time the spread haze of Florence below, that they realized luck had brought them in nothing more constructive than a huge circle. Rennie had at last agreed to stop and let Louise be the one to ask the way this time. With all available fingers stuck as bookmarks in the crisp new phrase book, and with a reckless confidence born of impatience with the baffling lanes, she'd tried her first words of Italian. *Per favore, Signora, dov'è Varetto?* The black-clothed woman with heavy stockings fallen around her ankles, who dangled a hen by the legs in one hand and held a cleaver in the other, had shaken her head as if in disapproval at the enquiry. She had muttered quickly, gesturing up and down the road with the flapping hen, bubbling out a reply which was none of those given in the book — *to the right, to the left, straight ahead, I don't know.* While Rennie stared in front of him and revved the engine loudly, Louise consulted the scrap of paper with Daniel's vague scrawled directions, and tried again. The woman's face split into a smile showing a single tooth in the middle of the bottom jaw, and the cleaver glittered as it pointed up the road and jabbed at the air.

— San Vincenzo, si si, a sinistra, sempre a sinistra!

Louise's thanks were obscured by Rennie's acceleration up the road, leaving the woman and her resigned drooping hen in the floating dust. Always bearing left, Rennie and Louise sped through tiny villages with long pious names, where all the shutters on the faded ochrous walls were closed against the sun. The roar of the engine in the narrow streets could have brought sleepy villagers in their vests to the windows, squinting through the shutters at the bright street and at the car with the steering wheel on the wrong side. For over a mile, across the side of a barren slope of olives, they were forced to grind along behind a tractor like a crawling bug, with a bright green umbrella attached to the back that swayed and fluttered with every rubbery bounce of the machine. Reflecting the umbrella, the driver's face was a luminous green and even his teeth were the colour of asparagus as he constantly turned in his seat, grinning and waving with flamboyant ambiguous gestures. Locked behind him, sweating in the cramped car, Rennie and Louise soon tired of smiling and waving back, and at last took the risk of becoming another statistic on these blind corners, overtaking the green farmer with a roar.

They'd looked in vain for the flags that Daniel had described, but Louise finally spotted the bare flagpole above the trees. As they slowed to negotiate the heavily rutted dirt road leading to the house where their host's children lived, Louise and Rennie were aware of how constricted they were in the car, and each wondered why the other had to give out so much heat.

They had hoped to be able to exchange brief greetings with Daniel's children and then be directed to the house in which they were to stay, the rustic one somewhere else on the property. But after ringing the doorbell again and again they had to come to the reluctant conclusion that Gabriel and Elena were not at home. As they stood wondering what to do, they had to cover their ears against the outraged barking of two dogs, baring their long yellow teeth and straining at the chains which held their necks close to the wall of the house. The hackles along their spines rippled as they jerked at the chains, and their barks seemed piercing enough to set off alarms or bring crowds out of the woods with rifles. As Rennie and Louise stared up at the windows of the second floor of the imposing house, they did their best to look like friends of the family, entitled to curiosity, rather than burglars looking for an unlocked entrance.

At the back of the house they discovered two small wild birds tethered to the ground by lengths of fishing line. The birds sprang repeatedly into the air, but each time their delicate legs were yanked almost out of the sockets and they fell back to the ground. Their efforts to escape had worn a circular bald patch in the grass, but they fluttered and dragged in silence.

Through the glass of the back door, Rennie and Louise could see the empty kitchen, as tidy and perfect as a decoy. One wall of the room was given over to twenty-four identical clocks that looked like the ones in railway stations that anxious travellers are so glad of. However each of these bland faces showed a different time. Seeing the clocks,

Rennie automatically pushed back his cuff to glance at his watch, while Louise listened at the glass. She held her breath, but her ears still hummed after the hours in the car, so that she couldn't decide whether the ticking she heard came from the clocks or from some weary mechanism in her head.

— Nice place, said Rennie.

He had taken off his watch to wind it but jumped backwards and almost dropped it as one of the birds blundered against his leg. With a furtive movement he bent down and wiped with a leaf at the runny white gob on his shoe.

The sun had left the front steps when they sat on them to wait, and the shadow of the house was reaching over the vineyards that sloped down the hill. Speaking over the snarls and intermittent barking of the dogs, Rennie and Louise discussed the possibility that the house on the ridge opposite — earth-coloured, crumbling — might be the one they were to occupy. However, Rennie pointed out, there seemed to be a house on the top of every ridge. He was so convincing they had almost persuaded each other that this was the wrong house altogether, in spite of the flagpole, when a dull grey van like a dog-catcher's approached up the driveway. They stood uncertainly, wondering whether their hosts had finally arrived or whether they were about to have a brush with Italian law. The windscreen reflected the sky so that whoever was inside was invisible, but when the door opened at last it was Daniel's children who stepped out. Even for siblings they looked remarkably alike, and their silence was like one person's. In spite of their youth they moved with the poise of a couple used to admiring stares, and their smooth Madonna-faces looked as if they could never pucker in either pain or laughter. Rennie advanced with confident outstretched hand.

— Hello, we're the Dufreys of course, I'm Rennie, and this is my wife Louise. Daniel told you we were coming?

The two calm faces seemed ready to deflect any amount of bonhomie, and although Gabriel smiled slightly as he shook hands, the nod seemed more one of resignation to the inevitable than an answer to Rennie's question.

— Yes, we were expecting you.

His boarding-school English was only faintly unbalanced to show the influence of his mother's language. Elena stared at Louise and said nothing, as if she only spoke Italian. There was a long moment in which all four stood looking at each other in silence, and in which Rennie's smile went flaccid. Elena finally spoke in the voice of an over-solicitous hostess.

— I expect you'd like to go straight to the other house.

Something about the long wait listening to the dogs made Louise speak quickly.

— Oh yes, I think that would be best.

The brother and sister started to say something at the same moment and exchanged a glance, then Gabriel said:

— Just continue the road, it's that house — see? — over there. You have the key don't you?

Rennie held it up, remarking jokingly on its resemblance to a dungeon key, speaking rather loudly as if to make the humour clear. Elena and Gabriel stared at him patiently. They seemed to expect neither pleasure nor irritation from their visitors, but were just determined to endure them. Rennie had lost faith in his little pleasantry when Gabriel said:

— I'll tell Domenico to bring you bread every day. There will be no need to pay him.

He added this quickly, as if payment would have been their first thought.

— He brings it to us in any case.

Rennie protested vaguely that they would pay, of course, but Elena was already moving towards the house and interrupted him to speak half over her shoulder.

— You must ask us if you need anything.

Gabriel moved away towards a shed beside the house. Further thanks and farewells seemed unnecessary, even inappropriate, in the face of this quiet disappearance, but when Rennie started the engine, its noise filled the silence with rude abruptness. As the hot little car bounced over ruts, Louise glanced back and saw Gabriel come out of the shed holding a scrap of bright cloth.

— Well they seemed nice enough, said Rennie, when we're settled we'll pay them a visit.

Louise didn't answer, and her doubtful nod was invisible to him as he slowed for a deep pothole.

— Don't you think?

Rennie refused to be discouraged when the key did not budge in the immovably rusted lock, and set off to look for a small window with Boy Scout resourcefulness and cheer. Louise picked her way through the blackberries after him, trying not to think about spiders and snakes, and wishing she had, after all, asked for at least a cup of tea from Elena. She could not stop herself from feeling watched, and glanced around uneasily as Rennie made up his mind what to do. He enjoyed smashing the window with the heel of his shoe, and Louise felt he regretted being too large for the hole. As she pulled herself through, she felt her palm slide across an edge of glass and cobwebs brushed her face. For a moment she was stuck halfway through the window and had to fight panic. Rennie called anxiously:

— You okay?

Her toes had finally located the floor and she had let

herself down, crouching as if expecting a blow, feeling the blood sticky between her fingers.

The plastic container of putty and the brown-paper-wrapped square of glass that they had bought in the village were still on the floor beneath the broken window. Louise hesitated at the door of the pantry, feeling its musty chill, but decided again that it could wait till tomorrow.

In preparation for the afternoon stroll — *mens sana in corpore sano*, as Rennie often reminded her — Louise took the chair from against the front door and pushed it half-closed, so that while they were away the goat would not come in and chew his way through *Jeremy Bentham: The Life and The Work of* The intimidating key was still wedged in the lock from their attempts to turn it on the first day, but they had not bothered to try to remove it since they discovered that the entire lock had crumbled away, and the door yielded like an eager virgin, at a determined push.

Louise sat down to wait for Rennie on the hot wooden bench outside, next to the row of dead plants in pots. When Daniel and his family had abandoned this house, had they given any thought to the lingering death these plants would suffer? Each time the heavy summer rain had cascaded from the gutterless roof, each plant must have yearned with all its energy to reach out from under the wide eaves and into the water. When there was wind as well as rain, some moisture must have reached the cracked earth in the pots to tease the plants with another few days of life. Now their dry stems rustled against each other and the long grass tickled Louise's legs.

She leaned back against the wall, where the flaking

plaster threw out its stored heat against her back. In the barn, Domenico's voice was winding itself up, gathering volume and vehemence in its slow acceleration towards the climax of midnight, when his voice would finally crack and fall silent. *E vero*, he was exclaiming. *E vero, e vero! Capito? Si, capito? Si si, capito?* As if in reply there came a soothing clucking of hens from inside the barn, like the automatic promises of a busy mother. When Domenico spoke again it was in long careful phrases as if elucidating a fine point of the case for the prosecution. Louise watched the rooster puffing out its scrawny feathers on a wheel of the hay-wagon and gathering its breath to crow, throwing its head back so the sharp pink bill within its mouth quivered. The pebble she threw missed, but hit the wagon close enough for him to scrawk and fluster down off the wheel and run behind the barn. Domenico's voice was low and dramatic now, with some deadly iron-fisted threat, or the tale of some mutilated corpse half-buried under the trees.

As Louise stared across the empty yard, the guinea-hen darted spasmodically out from the barn, its tiny round eyes glittering. Louise had not been able to decide whether there were several identical guinea-hens who only showed themselves one at a time, or whether there was only one. She watched closely, looking for some distinguishing feature in its egg-shaped spotted body. With many false starts and alarms, the bird made its way to the back wheel of the car. Louise heard Rennie's heavy tread on the inside stairs at the same moment that she realized why the bird was attracted to the wheel. She willed Rennie to be quiet as she watched the bird peck sharply, hopelessly, at its reflection in the hub-cap. As Rennie walked across the living-room, the bird snapped its reptilian head around to look, but could not resist a few more passionate pecks at its reflection before racing back to the barn as Rennie appeared at the door.

— You know those mice have moved the paper right away from the hole, he said. They must get together at night like a tug-o-war team.

Louise had to think what he was talking about, watching the guinea-hen huddled under a wheel of the tractor. Rennie walked around to the side of the house, where a skeletal ground-plan of broken walls, and a crumbled pile of masonry, indicated that at some point in the past, a portion of the house had caved gapingly, collapsed into itself, fallen. He climbed up on the remains of a wall and pointed.

— There's the hole. This is like a kind of ladder for them up the wall.

He kicked with his boot at the fallen wall, making a few stones collapse in a shifting of old mortar, and stared up at the house and the heavy grey moss hanging from the eaves.

— This whole place is going to go one of these days, he said, and slapped the wall as if testing it. After we've gone I hope.

He jumped down, flattening blackberry fronds with his boots, brushing grit off his hands.

— You ready to go? Thought we might go over to see those two today, Gabriel and what's-her-name.

Even in this warm afternoon, the wood in the valley between the two houses was as dark and clammy as a cellar used for growing mushrooms in rotten straw. Louise let go of Rennie's hand in the undergrowth, pushing against heavy dark bushes that almost obscured the path, knocking down unravelling webs strung loosely from branch to branch. Twigs dragged at her hair and a branch heavy with spines whipped into her chest behind Rennie. She let him thrust on ahead of her, listening to his body attacking each bush in its path like a flung-open door, heard him exclaim and slap away some insect on his face. The square cleaver would be useful here — that in one hand, the heavy bone-handled carving knife in the other, and the sap would run from every branch. When Rennie stopped suddenly and stood as if listening to military music or a bubbling cry of fear, the silence was full of tiny ticking sounds, the sudden shift of a disturbed leaf falling back into place over another, a sly rustle on the ground that might have been nothing more than a snapped twig settling into the earth. She heard the tightness in his voice:

— Darling let's get a move on.

Down here in the smell of moss and crushed leaves, the banality of the cuckoo's call was like a taunt.

On the far side of the wood, standing in the sun, they picked twigs from each other's hair, and Louise used a leaf to remove a tiny red spider like a furry pin head from Rennie's ear. Even when she had patted and rubbed herself, she felt sudden urgent pricklings on the back of her legs and her neck. In the long field running up to the other house, Rennie took her hand again.

— We'll go round by the road on the way back.

They walked awkwardly up the field together, Rennie's hand seeming to drag Louise forward at one step and impede her at the next so she found herself panting and stumbling. She imagined Gabriel and Elena watching their clumsy progress from behind the big windows.

— Maybe it's like the Queen, said Rennie. Flying the flag when they're at home.

Like the casual neighbours they tried to feel that they were, they knocked at the back door and heard the dogs bark inside the house. The birds were no longer fluttering and dragging at their lines, but the lines themselves were still tethered to the pegs in the ground. Louise bent to look closer and saw a knot like the ones that fishermen use, around a tiny stiff twig with clenched claws. Around the pegs, the earth had been worn down into a shallow dusty dish.

Elena opened the door and stared for a moment before smiling and stepping back into the house as if to show she had nothing to hide, smoothing the thick hair cut short across her forehead.

— How nice to see you, she said. Can I offer you a glass of wine? Or a cup of tea perhaps?

As they walked into the kitchen, Louise was aware of a quiet steady murmur, a low drone made up of hundreds of separate tiny sounds, and realized that each of the twenty-four clocks was ticking along with the rest, each one a busy mass of small agitated wheels beneath the bland face. Gabriel joined them in the kitchen, repeating his sister's gesture of smoothing the dark hair across his forehead as if concealing evidence. Elena screwed the corkscrew into the top of the bottle and handed it to Gabriel for him to draw out the cork. She held the glasses while he poured with a professional twist of the wrist, then handed her guests their glasses as Gabriel raised his in a toast.

— Salute.

— Cheers, replied Rennie, raising his glass. There was a pause in which he could clearly be heard swallowing. Louise remembered the way her mother's small talk bridged silences in company, and said in a rather high voice:

— This is good wine, is it local?

Gabriel held his glass up to the light and looked past it at her.

— Yes, he said. It's from a little village nearby.

— Really, maybe you'd take us there sometime?

Rennie was more animated than at any time since they'd left London.

— I'd like to buy some to take back with me to England.

He smiled at Gabriel but it was Elena who replied, pointing to the emblem on the label.

— The best kind of Chianti, she said. Gallo nero, this is what to look for, black cockerel, black rooster.

— Black cock, said Gabriel and they both took a sip of wine at the same moment. Rennie let out a short laugh and glanced at Gabriel as if about to wink at him. Gabriel didn't look at him, but shifted his chair around towards Louise, holding up the bottle to her.

— You see?

His finger pointed at the black rooster on the label and he watched her sideways. Elena leaned back in her chair and stretched so hard she appeared to grow several inches taller, then slumped down again, staring at the table with unfocused eyes.

— You tired? asked Rennie with indifferent politeness.

Elena shook her head without looking up.

— It's this heat, Rennie suggested.

— No, Elena said slowly. No, not tired.

She glanced at Rennie blankly, then stared across the table at Gabriel. He sat twirling his glass, untroubled by the three pairs of eyes watching him, grinning secretively like the dealer cutting the cards for another round.

There was a commotion at the door and the two dogs jostled in together, bouncing off each other and pulling away, their necks held close together by the short connecting chain.

— Down Lino, down Navero!

At Gabriel's shout the dogs squatted awkwardly together, jerking their heads against the chain.

— Nice dogs, Rennie suggested to Gabriel. Louise hoped he would not comment on the chain.

— Yes, said Gabriel without interest, they're good dogs I suppose. Our mother bought them as guards but now she has no need of them.

— Not with the Major, Elena yelped with a sudden uncontrolled giggle.

Louise knew that Rennie was about to say *What Major? What mother? And why the chain?* and filled the silence with the first thought that came to her.

— I like your flags, she said to Elena. They're like semaphore but I never learnt how to read it.

— Nor have we, Elena replied blandly. What they mean for ships is dull, I suspect.

Louise had the sensation of having flung back curtains only to find thick night outside. She watched the brother and sister exchange a glance.

— Daniel told us to look for the flags, she remarked. But we got thoroughly lost anyway.

Gabriel lifted the wine bottle to his lips, took a swig, and wiped his mouth with the back of his hand.

— Our father's directions were probably not too accurate. In some ways he's not very smart.

Rennie laughed uncomfortably as if suspecting a trap.

— Oh I don't know . . .

He laughed nervously, turned it into a cough and was silent. Louise said:

— His directions weren't too bad, but he told us to ask for Varetto and no one knew where that was.

Gabriel spluttered into his wine.

— Typical, he said. Not surprising you had trouble. He wiped his mouth and took another gulp of wine, leaving Elena to explain:

— Varetto is deserted, just ruins, no one's lived there for years.

Gabriel summed it up:

— Father's a bit out of touch.

— Well, we got here anyway, said Rennie. His voice was a little louder than necessary and carried on its edge a small weight of annoyance.

Gabriel and Elena leaned back in their chairs, letting Rennie's remark die in the silence. Louise picked up her glass to drink and tilted it to her mouth before she realized it was empty. Rennie turned to Gabriel as if to engage him in conversation but at that moment Elena said:

— Yes, you got here in the end. Perhaps you'd like to see the house.

She stood up and led the way out of the kitchen without waiting for an answer. Rennie followed with a backward glance at his wine — this invitation felt like the prelude to a polite goodbye — and Louise started out of the room after them, but Gabriel stopped her.

— It's boring up there. Let me show you my room.

His room, at the other end of the house, was large and sunny, looking over the valley towards the other house, which from this angle looked like a ruin, the crumbled stones and tiles of the collapsed end seeming to drag down the part still standing. How long would she have to stand at this window staring out before she would see it all crumble completely? The mice would be buried, the knives covered with tons of powdery stone and tile, and *Jeremy Bentham: The Life and The Work of*, would blow about, pages freeing themselves from the rubble and fluttering into the wheat.

— This is my collection.

Gabriel drew her away from the window to the dark side of the room. After the bright landscape and glaring sky, the corner he took her to was black and she squeezed her eyes tight, seeing darkness shot with rainbows. When she opened them she saw a bench at waist height and on it a kind of museum exhibit of stuffed birds. Louise put her hands in her pockets as if to keep them out of the way of the malevolent beaks and the threatening wings. One bird like a hawk gripped a mouse in its sharp claws. Where the talons were embedded in the preserved flesh, the pale belly was slit with a shining red gash.

— I touch them up for a better effect. More realistic.

As her eyes accustomed themselves to what they saw, Louise bent closer to examine each detail. A lizard as limp as string hung from one beak. In another sharp beak, the head and frenzied legs of a grasshopper still appeared to struggle. Like a tongue, a worm dangled from another clamped beak.

— These too, don't miss these.

Gabriel pointed to a further bench. Louise heard herself gasp as she saw snakes coiled around dead branches, each mouth open as if to strike and each split tongue protruding.

— There're very lifelike.

She wondered why she was whispering.

— Yes, not frightened are you?

She turned to see him watching her mouth.

— No, I'm full of admiration.

— Look, I'm proud of this one.

He stood behind her so that she could feel his breath in her ear as she stared at a thick snake that lay in a studied curl on a patch of sand with a bulge the size of a fist half-way down its length.

— They swallow mice whole. They love baby ones. Of course I had to get that effect in the mounting, but it's striking, don't you think?

He moved back to the window and stared out across the valley, humming and beating time with a finger on the pane.

— From here I can keep an eye on you.

Louise looked over his shoulder at their house and tried to remember whether the glass in the bathroom window was frosted. She felt herself blushing while Gabriel turned to watch her.

— Do you see anything interesting?

Gabriel pursed his lips as if considering.

— Sometimes I do. Sometimes, niente. Parla Italiano?

— Oh, poco.

She laughed and reddened more thoroughly.

— Molto poco in fact.

She laughed again and wondered why she was giggling nervously when he was so impassive. He broke the stare between them.

— My kingdom, he said. My desk. My bed. My stamp collection.

Louise saw that the bed was rumpled as if from a week of violent passion, but before she could decide whether the stamp collection was a joke, he said:

— Would you like to?

His eyes were a deep unflecked brown, so dark the irises were invisible.

— Learn, I mean.

He waited again and blinked several times while Louise licked her lips. He smiled.

— Italian, of course.

With a sudden theatrical swoop he took her hand and went down on one knee, declaiming in Italian. She wondered whether this had all been planned in advance, and stared at the spot like a navel on the crown of his head from which all the hair grew, and briefly imagined furtive passion in the hot hidden centre of a wheat field.

When he stood up and dropped her hand it was with as little expression as if he'd been tying his shoelace.

— Great language, he said dismissively.

He turned to the window and stared across the valley towards the other house. Louise thought he was shading his eyes from the glare with his hands but when she moved closer beside him she saw that he had made circles of his fingers and was looking through them like binoculars. She started to say something but as she did so he dropped his hands.

— Alora Louise, the others will be thinking we've run away.

He led the way back to the kitchen. There was still no sign of Elena or Rennie, and Louise found herself glancing up at the ceiling, waiting to hear a shoe fall to the floor above or a stifled giggle. Gabriel took a long gulp of wine from the bottle and wiped carelessly at the drops that spilled down the front of his shirt.

— I want to show you something.

Louise glanced guiltily toward the door. Gabriel caught her glance and said flatly:

— It's in here.

He opened the freezing compartment of the refrigerator and took out a small brown-paper package.

— See if you can guess what this is.

Feeling that something serious was involved in making the right guess, Louise took the frozen bundle, which had no particular shape beyond being thicker in the middle than at the ends. Like a child at Christmas she held it to her ear and shook it, smiling at Gabriel. The bundle didn't rattle and Gabriel didn't smile back.

— All this wrapping. It's not fair.

Gabriel shrugged and took another swig of wine.

— You know all you need to guess.

Suddenly impatient at all the obscurities in this house, Louise started to rip the paper away from the bundle, but Gabriel grabbed it from her. Louise did not know whether she and Gabriel had been staring at each other with the bundle held between them for a second or half an hour when Elena and Rennie came in. Elena looked at the bundle, at Louise, then at her brother.

— Showing our secrets?

Rennie crossed the room and watched as Gabriel unwrapped the bundle quickly and showed its contents to him like an Egyptian with a stack of postcards under his coat. The quick movement so obviously excluded Louise that she turned away to Elena, and as she did so she intercepted the shadow of a wink between the brother and sister. As if to smother the wink, Elena said quickly:

— You must come and see us again. Any time. When there are several flags up, that's a good time — means we're in a very good mood.

Gabriel let out a whooping laugh. Louise saw Rennie laugh too, glancing from Gabriel to Elena, and wanted to shout, can't you see we're not supposed to understand?

As she walked back down the driveway with Rennie, Louise felt the brother and sister watching them. She glanced back once and saw Gabriel take his hand from around his sister's waist and wave hugely like a fond uncle at an airport. Until they turned through the gate into the road, Louise continued to feel the stares in her back, and imagined the *sotto voce* remarks the brother and sister would be exchanging until their guests were out of sight, and the screams of laughter at their expense later that would make the dogs bark.

They walked back along the road, watching the sun expand milkily as it slid down towards the hills behind their house. Rennie spoke rather loudly into the evening:

— Those two are pretty weird. Daniel's such a tremendously good fellow, odd his children turned out like that.

Louise said nothing, but turned and walked backwards for a few steps looking at the two small flags fluttering above the trees. Rennie became more insistent.

— Don't you think?

She glanced at his heavy face, its every pore exposed in the last rays of sun, and was surprised by a dragging weight of boredom.

— Yes, she agreed, thinking of those two now, companionable over the wine in the kitchen, sharing an occasional joke.

— Yes, what was in the package?

Rennie kicked a stone along in front.

— Bit peculiar, some kind of bird. Frozen, you know, with the feathers and everything.

Louise concentrated on keeping out of step with him, walking in the other rut in the road.

— Can't imagine why he thought I'd want to see it.

She stopped and let him draw ahead, watching his oblivious back, wondering how long it would take, if she turned and walked back down the road, for him to be aware that she was no longer there, what she would say, exactly, when Elena opened the door with a glass of wine in her hand, quieting the dogs, staring in polite dismay?

— Listen, Rennie said, what happened . . .

He turned and found her not beside him and stood waiting, staring at his shoes, while she caught up.

— What were you doing with Gabriel all that time? That nutty sister was up to something, too.

Louise said nothing.

— Louise, I'm disturbed, you're being very strange.

He stood in the road with his hands in his pockets and his face thrust towards her, both belligerent and vulnerable in the direct light.

— He showed me his display.

Rennie's face flushed, or perhaps it was the red glow of the sun.

— His what?

— Stuffed birds and things, she mumbled. Like a museum.

She thought of the overgrown navel on Gabriel's head and his stern face as he stared through the imaginary binoculars. She and Rennie walked in silence. She glanced around at the trees, hearing invisible birds, with a sense of how close this landscape was to staggering crookedly into the sky, reeling in on itself, freezing and slivering apart in long thin shards. They continued to plod in silence and although she kept pace beside him, she imagined the sudden spurt of dust and the feeling of the breeze on her face if she tucked her elbows in to her sides and pelted up the road leaving him behind.

On the last stretch of road, where it followed the spine of the ridge, the darkening air filled suddenly with darting shapes too small and fast to see. Louise watched one of the tiny birds streak across in front of her, stop dead in the air for a suspended instant in which she saw the long flukes of a swallow's tail, and draw another straight line in the sky at right angles to the first. The air around their heads was full of clouds of midges hovering in a mass like a drifting clump of algae. The birds came at them from all directions, impossible to see, but hissing past them like a whip around their heads, making them flinch.

— What is this, Rennie said confusedly. What . . . ? He stood in a cloud of insects, straining to see into the dusk. Louise watched as three blurred shapes converged on him, watched him duck and cringe as if they were knives flying through the air. *Of course*, she thought, seeing him crouch with his hands instinctively raised around his face, *they're not attacking us, but in the dark an eyeball might seem as juicy a morsel as a midge.* He would stagger backwards, screaming, his hands over the blood pouring down his cheek, crouch with his head down, waiting for her to run over and help him, an arm around his shoulders and soothing words in his ear, to the house.

— Let's get out of here, he said in a high voice, and trotted heavily up the road out of the cloud of midges without turning to see whether Louise followed. She let him disappear around the corner of the barn and followed slowly, shuffling her sandals through the drifts of red dust on the side of the road, lingering, delaying the return to the house. The sun had set behind the interlocked hills and the sky was full of long shreds of cloud all drawn, like hairs down a plughole, towards the glow on the horizon left by the sun.

As she approached Domenico's barn, she wondered if he had been shouting as she and Rennie came up the road, and whether he was watching, waiting for them to go into the house before starting again. The barn seemed too silent, the split and peeling shutters sealed tightly on the window. In the dimness behind the shutters Domenico's eyes would be accustomed to the dark, and anyone walking across the yard would be exposed in every detail as he peered through the chinks, breathing quietly, watching. Louise glanced at the shutters and had to look away from the possibility that she was staring straight into his unblinking eyes, had to scuff a clump of straw along in front of her to obscure the sound of his unheard snigger as she passed, had to compose her face against his grimace in the gloom and the whispered Italian obscenities, who knows what it was he said? She winced as the low dim shape of the guinea-hen darted out and ran frantically ahead of her, flapping its wings against its sides as if being chased, or inviting pursuit. The house was very dark as she approached the front door, propped open again by Rennie, and she stood feeling the current of cool air from inside. In the loft the doves were murmuring soothingly as if telling each other calm bedtime stories. Louise saw a glimmering white shape in the opening above her and imagined the pungent warmth up there, and the odd white feather dislodged from under the armpit of a wing and floating down.

The house, inside, was rushing and humming with the flow of water. Louise sat at the marble table in the kitchen, imagining Rennie upstairs in the shower, obsessively soaping himself over and over, standing with the hair streaming down over his forehead, lathering between his legs with that look of satisfaction he had when tending his body. Louise prickled and itched all over as if she'd been rolling in long grass, so as soon as she heard the water stop flowing she went up to the steamy bathroom. Rennie didn't look at her as she came in and took her clothes off, but continued his methodical drying of each toe with his foot-only towel. Louise stepped into the stall and drew the curtain.

— I'm itching all over, she said. Were you?

— What? Rennie said irritably. Can't hear you.

Louise said in a much lower voice:

— You have a cut on your back.

— What? Where? What cut, I don't see it . . .

Rennie thrust open the curtain and she had an instant's prudish impulse to cover herself, perhaps because her body seemed invisible to him.

— Did you say cut? Do you see it?

The flesh of his back was soft and steamy from the shower and she thought how the skin could be pulled off smoothly along that translucent membrane between skin and flesh, leaving the bunched muscles exposed like an anatomist's model.

— No, I don't see it now. Must have been a shadow.

Rennie moved away to the mirror and she closed the curtain again. His crinkly hairs streamed over the soap and she held it under the water, rubbing at it with her fingers until all the hairs had washed away, listening to the reproachful or obstinate silence beyond the curtain. Hearing him rustle and sigh as he pulled his clothes on, hearing the snap of elastic against flesh, Louise parted the shower-curtain and glanced through, seeing that the big window in front of which Rennie was bending was of clear glass. Like this, at night, with darkness all around, the room would appear lit like a stage.

She pulled the shower curtain together, feeling the hot water gush over her shoulders, and closed her eyes. When she slid a finger up into herself she realized that the temperature of the water was exactly the same as that of her interior. She was smiling under the water, leaning against the wall, when her thumb felt some small hard protuberance in the pubic hair. The water was immediately too strong, too heavy. She fought against it rushing over her mouth and nose, and her eyes when she opened them couldn't clear the hair flowing down over her forehead. The small lump, like a scab, couldn't be pulled or scraped off with a fingernail and with sudden panic she bent forward trying to put her head between her legs to see what it might be. Water poured over the back of her head, rushed into her nostrils, and her hair streamed forward and hid everything.

Rennie was gone from the bathroom when Louise stepped out and squatted quickly on the floor, still dripping, with the hand mirror between her legs. The mirror kept steaming over, and drops of water landed on it, but each time she wiped it momentarily clear, she saw something small and black and possibly moving slightly, something that felt alive, definitely alive but embedded in her skin, something firmly attached but not part of her.

Naked, and leaving wet footprints on the tiles, she ran into the embryo room next door where Rennie was at the desk pushing back his cuticles. He glanced around with no expression and his eyes flickered briefly over her nakedness and then away.

— Rennie I'm sorry, Louise said, but there's something stuck to me. I can't see . . .

— Something what?

Rennie frowned at her as if listening to a stammerer.

— Would you mind looking, it's here.

Louise put one leg up on the chair next to him and felt the spot with her fingers.

— Here, look.

Rennie's face expressed nothing at all as he peered between her legs.

— No, here.

Louise pointed at the right spot. Rennie bared his teeth with sudden surprise and disgust.

— It's a tick.

He stared at her in horror.

— It's gone quite a long way in. I'll have to dig it out.

He didn't look at her or touch her but went into the bathroom and came back with tweezers and alcohol.

— Better lie down.

He spread a towel on one of the beds. As he worked in

160

her skin, his lips were drawn back and his eyes were narrowed like someone watching a wine-glass topple slowly from a high shelf and waiting for the crash. The alcohol stung and Louise felt the sharp ends of the tweezers gouging into her flesh, but she stared at the ceiling and forced her mind into that same empty trance as when, feet cold in the steel stirrups, she would feel the probing instruments and try not to imagine what the doctor might be doing between her legs, as the nurse would soothe with quiet meaningless phrases. Rennie was silent as he worked but finally straightened up and said:

— Think I got it all. It's bleeding a bit but I think I got it all out.

After a quick glance at her face, he took the handful of equipment back to the bathroom. Louise shuddered and gooseflesh rose all over her body. When Rennie came back she was running her fingers through her hair, feeling every inch of the scalp.

— I can't see my back, would you mind?

She turned slowly in front of him while he looked her over and watched impassively as she ran a finger down the cleft of her buttocks.

— No need to be paranoid, isn't one enough?

Louise had a headache and wondered whether it was from the tension of the last half hour, or whether the tick's poison was already circulating in her system.

In the bedroom she dressed slowly, hearing Rennie sneeze quickly three times from his desk but deciding not to say *Bless you darling* and hear him automatically reply, *Thank you darling*. She made no sound going downstairs and wondered how long it would take him to realize that she wasn't in the house.

A yellow light could be seen between the chinks of

Domenico's shutters, and a band of ground outside the door was illuminated. Looking at the light, Louise wondered whether Domenico had electricity in his barn or whether this syrupy light came from a lamp. As she moved closer she heard rustling from the room inside, and an occasional grunt. Both the barn and the house were very black against the still-pale sky and she stood for a long time watching the sky darken and the silhouette of the buildings become less crisp. Domenico's voice suddenly rang out, *Non e possibile! Non e possibile!* Louise had never heard Domenico from such close range and strained to interpret the rustling she could hear beneath his words.

Holding her breath and feeling suddenly congested from the thought of Domenico discovering her, she took a few steps closer towards the window and stopped in the abrupt silence. She could see that, to be able to look through the crack that ran across the shutter, she would have to climb on something. She waited until the silence was filled again with clattering and scraping noises. Domenico shouted in such anger that Louise was sure for a moment she'd been spotted. *Apra! Apra! Apra la bocca!* She wondered if this was abuse aimed at her. But his shouting gave way to a hoarse whisper: *Ecco, ecco, ecco.* She picked up a fruit box lying by the wall, and, moving only when he spoke, freezing in mid-movement when he was silent, put it under the window. From stopping and starting, and holding herself tensely rigid, she felt her muscles tight and, as she stepped quickly onto the box, under cover of a volley of shouts: *Aspetti! Aspetti! Aspetti!*, she felt a deep dragging spasm in her belly. Standing on the box in another sudden silence from within, she waited impatiently and when Domenico's voice rang out again she pulled up her skirt and thrust a hand inside her panties. Domenico fell silent and she stood bent over on the box with two fingers as far up inside her as they would go, not breathing, waiting for him to start again. *Basta cosi! Basta! Basta!* He sounded at his last desperate gasp. Louise jammed her fingers into herself hard, then carefully withdrew them and in the thick light from the crack in the shutter, inspected them closely. Along one fingernail and as far down as the first joint there was a definite dark smear. Letting her skirt drop back into place, she stared up at the sky and slowly released a long quiet sigh as if it was some days since she'd breathed.

La finisca! La finisca! Diavolo! Being careful not to let the box creak under her weight, Louise leaned forward until she could see into the yellow-lit stone room. At first she saw only chairs, at least a dozen of all shapes and sizes, lined up facing the window. She recognized three that had disappeared from the house. For a moment, seeing the chairs all facing her, she pulled back from the crack as if she had suddenly found herself on a stage, then looked through the crack again even more carefully. With the limited field of view the crack gave her, she couldn't see Domenico in the room, and had a moment's panic that he had crept out of the barn and was behind her, watching silently. But the dark yard was quite empty when she turned quickly to look, and when she heard him muttering from within the room she peered sideways through the crack, guided by his voice. By flattening her face against the peeling paint and squinting through one eye, she could just make out a pair of worn boots at the end of stretched-out legs and realized that Domenico was sitting on the floor with his back to the other side of the wall she was leaning against.

She continued to watch, and worked out the cause of the clattering and scraping when she saw the goat's hindquarters back slowly into her line of sight, and the legs agitate as if the animal was pulling against a rope attaching it to the wall near Domenico. *Basta, basta, basta.* His voice was a tired mumble. The goat's hindquarters remained still, the boots did not shift, and Louise was about to get down from the box when a hen strayed into the room by the door opposite her window, myopically pecking at a trail of straw under the chairs. Domenico suddenly leapt into full view, scattering the chairs as he kicked out at the chicken until it found the doorway again and disappeared into the dark barn beyond. Louise only just had time to jump down from the box and move it away from the window when Domenico came out of the barn, followed by the goat. She hoped she looked like someone who had just emerged from her house for an evening stroll.

— Buona sera, Domenico.

He stared at her before answering but it was too dark to see his face. After a moment he came toward her, grinning toothlessly, and spoke a few rapid sentences with many gestures. Louise had no idea what he was saying.

— Um . . . prego?

Domenico spoke again, gesturing more extravagantly, and this time she thought she heard the names of their neighbours.

— Gabrieli? Elena? Oh si, si.

Domenico came closer so that the light from the crack in the shutter illuminated him. He grinned and winked and spoke again through his grin. Louise understood nothing but when she shrugged and smiled in reply, he became impatient and repeated what he'd said, enunciating clearly and loudly.

— Il marito? Si, Rennie e suo marito . . .

But Domenico waved this away impatiently. Gesturing hugely and mouthing as if for the deaf, he pointed across the valley to the lights of the other house.

— Gabrieli. Elena.

Louise nodded. Domenico repeated his long sentence, but she still looked blank. He stared at her with open mouth, waiting for her to understand. His mouth let out a cackle without changing shape and he came even closer so she caught a whiff of some strong animal odour. He held up his hands in front of her face and watched her as he made a circle with the thumb and forefinger of his left hand and pushed the forefinger of his right hand in and out of this circle several times. He watched understanding suddenly blossom on her face, dropped his hands, and took a step back.

— Capisce? Capisce?

He winked at her heavily, made the gesture again, laughed hoarsely. Louise laughed as well and felt a sudden warm spurt between her legs that made her laugh even more. She repeated Domenico's gesture and he shrieked.

— Si, si, si!

As if disturbed by all the noise, the goat took a short skittish run across the yard. Domenico, still cackling, dragged it back by the rope round its neck. Pulling the animal behind him, he went to the box Louise had used and pushed it along the wall with his boot until it was once again where Louise had placed it under the window. He turned to her and gestured with his forefinger one more time, laughing with a noise like a hacking cough, then hawking and spitting into the weeds before dragging the goat back into the shed.

Upstairs Rennie was still at his desk in the Embryo Room. He didn't hear Louise as she climbed up onto the double bed and lay staring at the ceiling beam, a hand on her belly. She heard him tear up a sheet of paper and clear his throat, then turned over on her side, feeling a warm ooze between her legs, and pulled a pillow over her head.

She had been asleep, dreaming comfortably of a large green parrot hopping the length of a table, when Rennie shook her awake. Seeing his pale shocked face she sat up quickly.

— What is it?

Rennie pulled himself up on the bed and tucked his feet under himself.

— There's a snake, he said in a hoarse whisper. I saw its tail go under the bed, you know, where the mice . . .

He gestured towards the Embryo Room. The words came woodenly through his stiff lips and she saw from a great unconcerned distance that his eyes were blank with fear.

— It's been there all the time, he whispered in horror. I've been sitting there and it's been right there. All the time.

She stared at him, feeling herself smiling and her eyes widen with excitement. As she jumped down from the bed she cherished the spasm in her belly.

— Put your shoes on, she said briskly. And pull your socks over the cuffs of your pants.

She shook the galoshes in the wardrobe before pulling them on while he dragged his socks up. She ran downstairs, feeling a sudden hot spurt between her legs as she jumped down the last three steps, and took two brooms out of the closet. When she returned to the bedroom, Rennie was standing in the middle of the room, swaying slightly like a catatonic.

— That hole, Louise said, the one we thought was a mouse hole. Must be the snake's. We can scare him out through it and then block it properly.

In the face of his inertia her voice took on authority and when Domenico's was suddenly raised in aggressive emphasis from the barn it seemed to echo her own.

166

Louise led the way into the Embryo Room, half-hoping to see the snake whip out from under the bed and spend its venom striking its head again and again at the impervious rubber of her boots. Rennie took up position on the other side of the room, as far from the bed as possible. Louise didn't warn him that he was directly in front of the hole in the wall. She bent down to look under the bed and waited till her eyes had adjusted to the darkness under there, imagining the quick black streak across the floor, the sudden high scream from Rennie, herself rolling back the sock and seeing the two small holes on his ankle. The dark blot she could see now must be the snake.

— Careful, Rennie said, be careful Louise.

She glanced at him and saw him grip the broom tighter, holding it out in front of him as if to impale an attacker. His face was pale and seemed to have shrunk. Would the long zucchini knife be the best to lance the two poisoned holes, its own weighty determination as it fell across the flesh assisting her own last-minute faintness of heart? Or perhaps the slim flexible one, the sharpest of all, for two quick slashes as with a razor? Or perhaps the deep bite of the serrated one, whose tiny teeth would penetrate the flesh like a chainsaw through sappy bark?

— I'm going to prod it, Louise said. With any luck it will make for the hole.

As she jabbed the broom handle towards the dark shadow, she saw out of the corner of her eye that Rennie had realized the danger of his position. She saw him step quickly sideways and look for something to climb on. She would have to hold the ankle in her lap, so he couldn't see what she was doing, and keep the knives hidden from him. After the quick slashes, the wounds would not bleed for a moment as if shocked, and she would see grey beads of cartilage before the cuts would suddenly fill with blood. Just before Rennie climbed on the chair, she poked hard at the dark shape under the bed. She jumped back quickly and heard Rennie gasp. The dark shape did not move and there was no dark streak towards the hole. She jabbed again, watching it this time, jabbed and poked and pulled until the dirty blue shirt was lying at her feet.

— Oh my god, said Rennie, it could be anywhere.

Still standing on the chair, he lifted the broomstick off the floor as if the snake might suddenly dart out from somewhere and shimmy up it. Louise felt her feet hot and sweaty in the galoshes and felt the blood drying between her legs.

— It's probably gone already.

She went around the room carefully poking the broom under the other beds, separating the newspapers shuffled together in the corner, finally shaking both beds hard, until she saw the family under the plastic milling and agitating blindly.

— It's okay. It's gone for sure.

She took the brick Rennie used to keep the door open and put it against the hole.

— Locked out.

Rennie stepped down from the chair.

— Or locked in, he said.

They stood watching each other, hearing the scratching shuffle of the mice under the plastic. Domenico's voice carried clearly in through the window. The crowd was on its feet, waving banners, throwing caps in the air, and above it the voice gathered into a sonorous climax before it was drowned in wave after wave of cheers.